COWBOY OUTCASTS

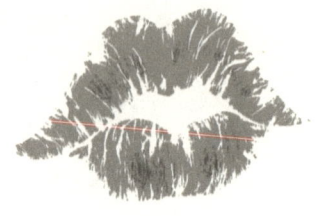

EVERNIGHT PUBLISHING ®

www.evernightpublishing.com

Copyright© 2020

Stacey Espino

Editor: Marie Medina

Cover Art: Sour Cherry Designs

Jacket Design: Jay Aheer

ISBN: 978-1-77130-185-5

COWBOY OUTCASTS

DEDICATION

I'm dedicating this book to my husband Marden and my youngest son Julian.
They both have to live with Tourette's Syndrome.
Hopefully, one day there will be a cure … or at least more public awareness.

COWBOY OUTCASTS

COWBOY OUTCASTS

Stacey Espino

Copyright © 2012

Chapter One

Tourette Syndrome (TS) is a neurological disorder characterized by tics: involuntary, rapid, sudden movements or vocalizations that occur repeatedly in the same way. The cause has not been established and as yet there is no cure.

"Ms. Watson, I don't have time for this now." Carl Fischer adjusted his glasses as he continued down the hallway of the university. Hailey tagged along behind him, balancing a pile of heavy textbooks in her arms.

"Sir, please. I need more funding for my research. If you read my proposal, you'd see the validity of what I'm trying to achieve."

The professor turned a corner, keeping up his hurried pace. "Everyone's proposal has validity, Ms. Watson. The university would be bankrupt if we funded every shining star."

One of her books dropped to the ground. She struggled to pick it up, attempting to bend down without spilling the rest of her load. The professor had made it to the other end of the hallway, about to escape into the stairwell. "Sir! The hogs are going wild. Something has to be done."

He pushed open the door and then turned to face her. "Then I suggest you find a way to deal with it. *Without* university funding." The door eased shut behind him, leaving her standing alone in the quiet hallway. She never expected him to agree. She'd already applied for every grant in the state, to no avail.

Hailey exhaled, her shoulders slumping as the slim hope she'd held onto faded away into nothingness. The right side of the hallway was all windows, looking down onto the courtyard. She set her bundle on the ledge and watched the students walking along the various paths. Only two years ago she was doing the same thing, rushing to classes, studying day and night. Some days she didn't know why she bothered at all, but then she'd remember her research. Understanding the human mind was her passion, and she wanted to take it as far as possible. But until now she'd only dealt with horses and dogs.

Hailey quickly learned that a Master of Science did not equate to a six-figure income. In fact, she barely made enough to pay her rent at the boarding house. She wouldn't complain if they'd only give her enough money to continue her animal behavioral research. Her options became fewer each day.

She made her way to the parking lot. Her old jalopy waited for her in the same spot every day, its mix of rust and layers of old paint making it the talk of the campus. Luckily she was usually the last to leave each day because her pickup was in desperate need of a new muffler. The two mile drive to the boarding house was enough to wake the dead.

"Hales, wait up!" Peter ran across the parking lot towards her, waving a few pages of paper.

She dropped her research books into the bed of her truck and waited. Peter was a good friend. He'd graduated alongside her, but his focus was on agricultural management and pest control. "What is it?"

He was slightly winded, bending over to catch his breath. "I thought these might interest you."

She took the papers from him. "What are they?"

"They were posted in the local feed shop just south of here. I thought it would be a good way for you to do your research…on a budget."

She smirked. "You knew Fischer would say no, didn't you?"

Peter shrugged. "I feel bad. It's not fair that my project got funded and yours didn't."

"That's because there's money to be made in your case. The pesticide market is huge around here," she said. "Besides, I'm glad at least one of us got funding. One day I'll be able to say I was best friends with a Nobel Prize recipient."

"Sure, Hales," he scoffed. When a distant group of students called out his name, he tapped the papers he'd given her and started jogging down the manicured lawn. "I'm booked to tutor a group of second-year chemistry students. Five minutes ago."

"Thanks, Pete. See you tomorrow."

Hailey climbed up into her truck and slammed the stubborn metal door shut. She sorted through the papers. Several local ranchers had placed ads in the feed store requesting professional help to rid them of their pest problem. Most sought archers and huntsmen. The need only confirmed what she'd been trying to prove to her superiors—hogs were having a major negative effect on the farming industry in their state. There had to be a better balancing act between keeping the animals safe and the farmers profitable. It seemed like the perfect symbiotic relationship. Hailey would be able to conduct hands-on research in the field, and she'd hopefully be able to help a farmer save his crops.

****

"You seen that brother of yours lately?" asked Howard.

"Uh-uh," said Callum. He scanned the ads on the bulletin board in the feed store, not paying much attention to the owner.

"How long's it been now?"

"Nearly a year since I last saw him," he said dismissively. "You take down my ad, Howard?"

"I never touch the board. There was a student in here yesterday asking about fertilizer and pesticides. One of those tree-huggers from the university. He took a few ads with him."

"The whole damn ad?" Callum ran a hand through his hair, wondering what a student would want with his advertisement. "Now I'll have to print off another copy."

"Don't be too hasty. I know plenty of ranchers who got free services through the university. Their students are just itching to get their hands dirty."

"They could help with my hog problem?"

"Can't see why not. Unless you have top dollar to pay a professional, you can't go wrong using a student."

He pondered the idea as a couple entered the store, the glass bells clanging against the glass door. They made a wide arch around him, not making eye contact. He stood tall, staring them down until they reached the other end of the aisle.

Three, two, one. One, two, three. Three, two, one.

Howard came from around the counter and whispered, "Callum, you're grown now. Overgrown, if you ask me. You're intimidating when you look at people like that. How do you expect to make friends?"

He scoffed. "I don't need friends. Certainly not the likes in this God-forsaken town."

The older man tsked, shaking his head. "I don't know where you steered wrong but your parents wouldn't approve."

Three, two, one. One, two, three. Three, two, one.

"You think the lovely townsfolk have been good to us? They treat their fucking livestock better."

"Lower your voice," he whispered harshly. The only reason Callum allowed Howard to speak so forward was because he'd been one of the few rocks in his life. He'd taken Callum and his brother under his wing after their parents died over a decade ago. He wasn't sure why the old man bothered to care. Nobody else did.

Callum's cheek began to twitch, signaling it was time for him to make his exit. He had to get his nerves under control before they controlled him. The stares and whispers were nothing new. And worrying about his ranch wasn't going to help anyone. Born and raised a cowboy, he knew only steadfast hard work would change a thing.

Everything just seemed to be adding up lately, and he was doing it all on his own since Arden took off. Each time he found a section of his crops destroyed by hogs, he felt powerless to protect them. He couldn't be everywhere all the time. His land was vast, and he needed to sleep, even for just a few hours a night. Expensive surveillance equipment and fencing were out of the question, and he didn't have the experience to hunt the hogs down, bringing him back to square one. He needed help, and he needed it free.

"I'll bring a new ad by tomorrow," said Callum, dipping his hat as he turned to leave.

"Call the university. It's worth a try."

He left the claustrophobic confines of the feed store, taking a deep breath of country air—a mix of pine, barley, and burning wood. The feed store was located on the periphery of town, the last stop before the open road.

If no one would help him, he'd have to help himself. He planned to set traps. Lots of them. He wouldn't watch his crops go to hell because of the unchecked hog population. It was difficult enough running things without Arden, so he didn't need any added headaches.

The booming sound of bass neared as he walked along the side of the road towards his truck. He didn't bother to turn around.

"Hey, retard, stay out of town!" shouted one of the men in the pickup as it passed. His blood boiled. Jeremy and his friends had been a thorn in his side since grade school. Callum was twenty-nine now, not twelve. He should be able to control his temper and ignore such ignorant pricks, but he couldn't let it go. His anger enhanced the twitch in his face, and things would only get worse now that his anxiety levels spiked.

If Arden were in town, he'd have hunted them down and given them a taste of cowboy justice. He struck out first and asked questions later. Callum only retreated more into himself.

Three, two, one. One, two, three. Three, two, one. He'd taught himself years ago to use number combinations to stay focused, to keep his Tourette's at bay. Sometimes it worked—if he was lucky. When it really counted, nothing seemed to help him appear normal. Women often referred to him as a pig wearing cologne because they'd be attracted to him only until they found out about his problem. Older generations would quote the Bible, Mark 5:1-20, saying he was demon possessed with all his crazy animal noises. If he never had to come into town at all, he wouldn't.

Jeremy didn't realize he was playing with fire. Some days were more difficult for Callum to rein in his temper than others. Like the townsfolk frequently said, he was an animal, a freak of nature. He made people uncomfortable so they didn't want him around.

The truck revved its engine, burning rubber as it peeled down the street, the music fading into silence. He sighed a breath of relief.

Callum settled in the driver's seat of his truck. He drove the dusty back roads home, the rough surface doing a number on his suspension. He had to haul the rusty bear traps out of the hay loft and get them oiled up in addition to his usual work load. His mind processed so much at once. He had plowing to get done, fences that needed mending, and wood to split. Without Arden, he was a one-man crew, everything falling on his shoulders. But unlike his brother, he refused to abandon the family ranch. All their memories were preserved within the walls of the house.

Every night when he'd sit alone in the living room watching the flames dance in the fireplace, he'd reminisce about his parents. His father used to tell them about Ireland in the evenings, using his gift of storytelling to make the recounts fun and interesting. Whenever things got tough on the ranch—drought, flooding, lack of resources—his father would always compare their misfortune to life back in the homeland. After hearing the tales of true famine and suffering, Callum and Arden learned to keep their mouths shut and give thanks no matter what the circumstances. They'd study the Bible as a family, something Callum still did on his own.

Now he was alone—no parents, no brother, not even a friend in the world. Maybe God was punishing him for taking his family for granted when he had them. But blaming himself wouldn't change the facts. He had to carry on, one day at a time.

Callum kicked off his boots and tossed his Stetson on the coffee table after arriving home. He was still pissed off because of Jeremy and needed to clear his head for a while. He dropped down in his favorite worn chair and massaged his temples. The only sounds in the lonely house were the drip of the kitchen faucet and the grandfather clock's rhythmic ticking. He watched the pendulum, reminded of his mother. She'd brought the family heirloom all the way from Ireland when she came to the country. It was her pride and joy. No matter how rough times got, his father would never consider selling it. And Callum never would, either.

Just as the throbbing in his head began to subside, the telephone rang. It was such a rarity to hear that he jerked in his seat, looking back and forth before realizing it was just the phone. He hoisted himself up to answer it.

"Hello, is this Mr. O'Shea?"

"Who's asking?"

"I saw the flyer you posted in the feed store," said the girl.

He frowned. "So you're the one stealing ads. You're supposed to write down the number, not take the whole paper." He didn't mask the irritation in his voice. There was no one in the world left to impress.

"I may be able to help. With your hog problem, that is."

"Unless you have some magical elixir that'll wipe

out the hog population for good, I don't see how a little girl from the university can possibly help me."

"I'm not a student. I'm a specialist in animal and human behavior."

"Well that certainly sounds too fancy for me. I can barely buy oats for the horses, never mind pay some overpriced scientist who—"

"I won't charge you," she interrupted.

"Nothing's free, sweetheart. What's the catch?"

"I'd like the chance to study the animals firsthand, in their natural environment. I need to learn more about them in order to make sure they don't pose a problem for humans."

He really wanted to tell the girl to fuck off and bother someone else. But if she could help him get rid of the hogs at no cost, he'd be a fool to say no. "How long will this take? A day? Two?"

She chuckled as if he'd said something funny. "Weeks. Possibly months. I need to monitor their habits, conduct tests, get into their heads. I wouldn't take up much room. I'm fine sleeping in the barn if it's livable. All I need is a cot."

"Live here?" He hadn't expected that gem. "Nobody lives here but me. I'm not keen on hosting a National Geographic party, and certainly don't have time to babysit you." With that he hung up the phone and returned to his chair. The nerve of that girl, expecting a free ride for Lord knows how long. He needed the hogs gone now, not in a week or month. Tomorrow he'd clean up the bear traps and do things his way.

Chapter Two

Hailey had to find a better way to appeal to Mr. O'Shea. Cowboys in the area were so set in their ways that it was difficult teaching them anything new. The other ads she'd responded to had no interest in preserving the hogs. They wanted them all wiped out and roasting on a spit. Half the men were in the Stone Ages in the way they cared for their own livestock. It could get inhumane, even barbaric—she'd witnessed it with her own eyes during her training.

Her line of work gave her an intimate look into the mind of an animal. They weren't much different than people when stripped down to the basics. It was her goal to ensure man and beast cohabitated peacefully, but half the battle was getting pig-headed cowboys to listen. Or universities to sponsor her research.

It was less than two weeks until her money ran dry. She'd worked in the lab all winter, assisting the chemists with their dirty work. Now the semester was coming to a close and she was no longer needed. No money meant she had no way to pay her room and board. She couldn't ask her parents for a handout because they didn't approve of her choice not to follow tradition and practice medicine.

Hailey was going to try and get tutoring jobs like Peter but even the students would be off for break soon. She had to get herself set up on a ranch doing research or she'd been homeless. If she could prove any of her theories in the field, she could write up a convincing proposal for funding. With solid evidence to back her up, she was confident they'd finally see the validity of her work.

The next day after she left the campus, she drove out to the local diner. Carrie, the fulltime waitress, knew just about every piece of juicy gossip ever to grace the small town. She'd know the address to the O'Shea Ranch. Hailey knew she'd have a better chance of convincing Mr. O'Shea of her offer if she could talk to him face to face. He'd see firsthand that she wasn't imposing, wouldn't even take up much room.

It was lunch hour when she entered the diner. Dirty and dusty cowboys lined the counter and several booths held university students. It was an odd mix, one she'd never find in the city. But without her parents to finance her education, she had to accept the scholarship to the much lesser-known university right in the middle of the prairies.

"Mornin', sweets. What can I get you?" asked Carrie. She looked to be about forty, her long blonde hair gathered in a ponytail.

"I was wondering if you could do me a favor…and I'll have an iced tea." She sat on the furthest swiveling stool, out of earshot from the men.

Carrie set her drink down, the moisture on the cup reminding Hailey that today was supposed to reach record highs.

"What do you need?"

"I need the address to the O'Shea Ranch. Not for anything bad," she assured. "I just wanted to talk with the owner about work."

The woman shook her head, a concerned frown on her face. "You don't want to do that. Haven't you ever heard of the O'Sheas? They're nothing but trouble, I tell you. Those boys are a menace, only looking to pick a fight."

"They posted about a hog problem."

"Well, be smart and let them worry about it. Arden hasn't even been into town in ages. Rumor has it he's a no-good, drunken drifter now. And Callum…Good

Lord, you want nothing to do with that animal."

After listening to more of her complaints, Carrie mentioned they lived just past the bridge off the east side of town. Hailey stored the information to memory, finished her iced tea, and then made her way to the O'Shea Ranch without a second thought.

Her truck droned loudly, scaring away flocks of blackbirds in the fields as she past. Although she'd taken her bachelor's degree in the city, she'd spent the past four years at the university—two studying and two working for less than minimum wage. In all that time, she rarely ventured off the grounds. There was mostly farmland beyond the campus, nothing to see, and everything worthwhile too far to drive to.

The O'Shea Ranch was the only house within miles, so she knew she had the right one. The house itself looked unkempt. If it weren't for the clothes on the line, she'd assume it was abandoned. Grass grew tall around the house, weeds reclaiming the walkway. A measure of foreboding entered her heart as she stepped out of her truck. The waitress's words played in her head, making her wonder if it was a mistake coming here at all.

"Hello?" She walked around the side of the house, carefully watching her step. The screen door was slapping against the frame, the main door open. She bent down and peered inside before knocking. Beyond the entrance was a country-sized kitchen with a heavy oak table. She expected a disaster after viewing the property, but there were only a few dirty dishes on the counter. It was all very basic, lacking a woman's touch.

The sound of a rifle being cocked made her gasp. She nearly toppled over but found her balance at the last second. "Trespassing?"

"I–I called…yesterday…about the hogs. Are you Mr. O'Shea?"

The cowboy was not what she expected. He towered over her 5'3" frame, all sinewy golden muscle. His Wranglers were too low on his hips to be holy, his chest bare and sweat-glistened. After resting the barrel of the rifle on his shoulder, he tilted his black Stetson back. "You're the student?"

"Scientist." She felt completely intimidated.

"You're lucky you weren't shot. We don't take kindly to intruders around these parts. There hasn't been anyone brave enough to cross my property line in too many years to count." His voice was deep and gravely, his eyes narrowed in distrust.

"I just wanted to talk. I meant nothing disrespectful." Surely he had some decency. She couldn't imagine any man being as callous and crude as Cassie had described.

He started to walk away from her, towards the large century barn. He spoke without turning around. "I thought I made myself clear on the phone. I haven't the time or money to have you underfoot. I'll kill the hogs with my traps and be done with it."

"You can't do that!" She ran up ahead of him and walked backwards so he'd have to face her. "Killing isn't the answer, Mr. O'Shea. There are better, more humane ways of handling the problem."

"Your ways take too long, little girl." He brushed past her. His accent was slight but undeniable. She'd always been a sucker for an Irishman.

"There's no harm in trying. I won't be a bother," she said, trying to keep up with his long strides.

He reached the bay doors of the barn and disappeared into the first stall. As he backed out a chestnut quarter horse, he continued to talk. "And I suppose I'll be expected to feed you as well?"

The cowboy stroked the horse's neck lovingly, a

look of concern on his face.

"I promise, I don't eat much."

He continued to examine the horse. "I knew there'd be a catch," he said, moving to the other side of the animal. "There always is."

"Is there a problem with him?"

He glanced over at her briefly. "He's recovering from Choke. Third time it's happened."

"Have you tried putting oversized rocks in his food trough? It'll force him to eat slower."

He smacked the horse on the rump, sending it through the open gate towards the grazing pasture. "How you know so much? You don't look like any cowgirl I've ever seen."

"I'm not. But I've learned a thing or two along the way. I did a year on equine studies," she said. "And by the way, I'm not a little girl. I'm twenty-sex."

"Are you now?" His interest suddenly piqued. He cocked an eyebrow and ran a hand along the stubble on his jawline.

Hailey blushed, realizing her Freudian slip. "Twenty-six. I meant, twenty-six."

"I suppose you could stay in my brother's room. I doubt he'll be back."

"Do you live alone here?"

"I do."

She glanced around the landscape, wondering how one man could maintain so much acreage. Why was he alone? He certainly wasn't hard on the eyes—or any of the senses. The man even smelled good, a mix of leather, horses, and clean sweat. As she discreetly took in every hard ridge of muscle, she realized that eight years had passed since she started her first year of secondary education. In all that time she'd never dated, never thought about a future beyond her career. It took only a few minutes alone with Mr. O'Shea for her body to respond, reminding her she was a woman, not just a scientist.

She realized they hadn't introduced each other properly. Calling him Mr. O'Shea her entire stay would be a bit much. "My name's Hailey Watson, by the way." She held out her hand.

"Callum." After a brief shake of the hands, he closed the gate and walked back in the direction of the house. "You should get a new muffler for your truck."

"I would if I could afford one."

"Aren't scientists supposed to be rich?"

"Apparently not my branch. If I were in this for the money, I would have called it quits years ago."

"Makes no sense to me," he muttered as he entered the side door to the kitchen. She wasn't sure if she was expected to follow him in or wait outside, so she stopped at the threshold.

"Ms. Watson, you gonna stand there all day?"

She quickly opened the screen and entered, feeling out of her depth. "Please call me Hailey. My professors all call me Ms. Watson, and it makes me cringe when I hear it."

"It's your name, no?"

"We may as well be on first name basis. I won't be able to solve the hog problem overnight."

"Hailey." He said the word slowly, enunciating every syllable with his Irish tongue. The sound traveled through her body like a charge of electricity. The way he made her feel staggered her. "We have this name back home, too. It means hay meadow, just like the one to the west of the house."

"That's not very romantic," she said.

"You haven't seen the field as the sun rises or sets. You'll change your mind after that." After he spoke, he set his cowboy hat on a hook and then ran a hand through his thick, dark hair. He rarely made eye contact, which she found odd. His eyes were as dark as onyx and she wondered what was hidden in their depths. There must be more to this man than rumors and an empty house.

She tentatively walked around the kitchen and then entered the living room. There was a massive stone fireplace, an oak grandfather clock, and a few pieces of mismatched furniture. The old recliner was positioned right in front of the hearth, and she couldn't help but picture Callum spending long, lonely nights in that chair. It wasn't natural for humans to live alone, just as it wasn't natural for most animals.

He certainly didn't sit around and mope too much because his body carried no extra fat, just solid, lean muscle. When she glanced behind her, he was standing still in the entryway of the room, his arms crossed over his bare chest. He watched her in silence, like a predator studying its prey before the takedown. Was she in danger being alone here with him? Carrie had warned her. Would she regret not taking the advice she assumed was gossip? Hailey commended herself for having an open mind. It was the only way to tackle science or life in general. She liked to make decisions based on facts and personal experience, not hearsay and gossip.

So far she didn't know what to make of the dark-haired Adonis. He was rough around the edges, curt, and antisocial. But he'd agreed to give her the opportunity to work his ranch knowing he'd have to provide food and shelter. That was a big bonus point in her books, so they were off to a decent start.

"It's a big house for one person," she said after walking the perimeter of the room. There was a staircase heading to the upper level and a hallway leading to another area of the main floor.

"My brother only left last year, but I still wouldn't sell it for all the money in the world." There was an inflection of defensiveness in his tone. He continually blinked his eyes and she wondered what it meant.

"I think that's admirable."

He cocked his head to the side. After studying her for a moment, he waved for her to follow him. "Come. I'll show you your room."

The stairs were creaky, testimony to the house's age. She had no fairy tale memories of childhood—creaky steps, nights by the fire…love. Callum, however quiet, seemed to be holding onto a great legacy, memories worth cherishing. She envied him for that. Her family was sterile and materialistic, both qualities she loathed.

He had to kick the bottom of the warped door for it to open. "I haven't been in here in months," he said. "No need."

She walked past him and looked around. The bed was made in a patchwork quilt. Everything was preserved as if he either expected his brother to return or didn't have the time to pack everything up. There were photos on the wall, cologne bottles on the dresser, and trophies lining a tall wooden shelf.

"What are these for?" She ran a finger along the thick dust covering one of the trophies.

"Rodeo riding. I suspect that's what he's doing now, but I wouldn't know."

"Is he older than you?" she asked.

When he didn't answer after a few moments, she turned around to gauge his reaction. He looked tense, his facial muscles twitching and jaw clenched. Had she said something wrong? His brother must be a sensitive topic.

"Three years older," he finally said. He turned his back to her. "Washroom is at the end of the hall. My room is next to it if you need anything." Then he took off without another word. At least there wouldn't be any funny business going on. The man appeared to be repulsed by her. She was a problem he barely tolerated. Once the hog invasion was remedied, she was sure she'd get a swift kick in the ass off the property.

It shouldn't matter one way or another. She was at the O'Shea Ranch for a purpose—to continue her research and make it through another day. But there was something dark and alluring about the Irish cowboy that pulled her in. She wanted to get into his head, like her animal subjects, and learn everything there was to know about him besides the fact he had a nice ass.

It felt like butterflies fluttered in her stomach, awakening her dormant sexuality. Now the challenge would be ignoring her human nature, which suddenly reared its ugly head. Science was so much easier without unexpected variables.

Chapter Three

Callum managed to avoid the girl the rest of the day and evening. As the sun set he returned from the fields, exhausted and hungry. He wasn't used to having another person to care for. He'd have to get used to the responsibility while she was there. With little daylight left, he'd have to settle for barbequing up some of his frozen chickens as fresh would take too long to prepare.

He hoped he'd be able to control himself around her this round. His Tourette's seemed to run rampant when he was in close proximity to the little blonde. Why? He had nothing to prove and certainly wasn't attracted to her. She'd likely turn out like all the others—disgusted by him given enough time. But she offered a free service which he wasn't in a position to refuse. He blamed his nerves on his solitary lifestyle. He just wasn't used to having someone else around.

When he entered the kitchen, the lights were off. He needed to start a fire inside to stave off the evening chill, and one out back to prepare the food.

"Hailey?" Had she gone to sleep already? Guilt began to well inside him. The girl was already too thin in his opinion, and now he was starving her.

After no response, he ran up the stairs and checked all the rooms. Where the fuck was she? Her truck was still parked in the lot, an unpleasant eyesore. He knew he'd end up playing babysitter.

"Hailey?"

He grabbed his padded jacket from the coat tree and headed to the barn. There were acres of wheat and hay fields around the house, so he'd be sure to find her if he patrolled the area on horseback. The forests were a distant line on the horizon, too far for her to venture, and the breeding ground for those damn hogs.

Callum cantered around the area for nearly half an hour with no sign of the girl. He was about to turn back when he heard a remote scream. It came from the forest, now shrouded in night.

He jabbed the heels of his boots against the horse's sides and galloped through the blackness. The sense of urgency made his heart race, adrenaline pumping through his veins. Wind rushed through his hair, burning his eyes. He strained to see with only the gentle cast of moonlight. The soft glow highlighted the waves of wheat that surrounded him like a golden ocean.

As soon as he reached the treeline, he dismounted before bringing the horse to a full stop. "Hailey!"

"Callum!"

He pulled his rifle off the side of his saddle and ran blind towards her voice. Her whimpers spurred him on, helping him find her with increased ease. She was bunkered down behind some unruly briars. The yellow, glowing eyes of an oversized hog were the source of her distress. It was an unruly beast, choosing to attack rather than retreat. Its feral growl warned Callum to stay back.

It was too dark to aim his rifle with certainty. He dropped it to the ground, pulled a blade from his boot and charged forward with a roar of his own. The hog was powerful with lethal tusks attempting to rip him to shreds. Unfortunately for the hog, this wasn't his first wrestling match. They struggled, rolling about on the forest floor. The roots and briars scraped his exposed face and jabbed him in the ribs. They danced until Callum found the moment to strike, driving the sharpened blade into the animal's throat, slicing wide. It took a few moments for the wild boar to finally settle, its life ebbing away.

He lay there on his back with the moonlight filtering down through the forest canopy, his breathing rapid and heavy. As soon as his wits returned, he shoved the dead weight off him, stood, and went to collect the girl. He snagged her wrist, yanking her out of the brushwood and pulling her along behind him. Without a word, he hoisted her up onto his horse, grabbed his gun, and mounted behind her.

The ride back across the fields was uneasily quiet. Only the rhythmic beat of the horse's hooves and Hailey's occasional sob could be heard.

Once back home, he helped her dismount and immediately brought the gelding to the barn for unsaddling. He hated pushing his horses this late at night, and he blamed Ms. Watson and her foolhardy expedition.

"I'm sorry," she whispered. He didn't realize she was behind him in the barn.

"You should get inside before you catch a chill." If he dealt with her now, he'd regret it…or at least she would. His mother had always told him to take a walk or go for a ride before addressing the object of his irritation. Speaking from a right mind didn't land a man in boiling water nearly as often as acting out of passion. His father and brother never understood that concept, giving the O'Shea men a bad reputation.

"It's just that you were gone, so I thought I'd start my research. I didn't expect the sun to set so fast. Then—"

"You're lucky you weren't killed! Those hogs could have gored you to death. And I could barely find you in the darkness. Foolish all around."

"I'm sorry," she repeated. "And thank you for saving me."

After reluctantly putting his horse away wet, he closed the bay doors and marched back to the house. Little Ms. Watson could be sorry all she wanted, but the woman was already proving to be more trouble than she was worth.

"I'll cook some chicken for you," he said as he walked.

"That's okay. It's late, don't bother."

"I said I'd feed you. Regardless of your little stunt, I won't have you go hungry."

"I don't eat meat…or chicken."

He stopped dead in his tracks, only a few feet from the door. "How do you expect to live? All I cook is meat. This ain't some fancy vegetarian buffet."

"I'm not trying to be difficult."

Callum flicked on the lights after they entered the house. The first thing he noted, when he could see with perfect clarity, were the scrapes on Hailey's knees. Any cowgirl in her right mind would have worn Wranglers out on the fields, not little cotton shorts. He didn't know what to make of her. She lived in the tiny town but knew little about country living—besides her book learning.

"Sit down," he said, leaving no room for argument.

She complied, lowering into one of the wooden chairs. There used to be a family member occupying each of the hardwood seats. Now it was just him.

"I'm okay," she said, wincing when he attempted to touch the bloody scrapes.

He shook his head and went to collect the medical kit from above the fridge.

Callum was used to taking care of himself. He'd broken a rib a few years back. Arden had bound him tight and the wound healed without the need to visit an overpriced doctor. Many of their injuries over the years were brawl-related as opposed to accidents working the ranch. They were two to be messed with before Arden decided he wanted more out of life and moved out. It seemed his brother took Callum's courage with him when he left.

He carefully dabbed at her knees with iodine on a cottonball as he crouched in front of her. Callum noticed her legs weren't half bad, long for a woman of her height. When he'd glance up to see if she was in pain, her big, blue eyes were crystalline with unshed tears.

"What's done is done," he appeased. The last thing he needed was a woman crying her eyes dry in his house. He wouldn't have a clue how to comfort her. Women were a rare commodity in Callum's life. The townswomen rejected him on sight, and the last time he'd travelled to the city for a one-night stand was when Arden still lived at home.

"I should have waited 'til morning." She sucked air in through her teeth as he cleansed her wounds. "It won't happen again."

"Damn straight it won't. In fact, maybe it's best if you head back to the university tomorrow morning."

"No," she snapped. "Please…please give me a little time to prove myself."

He grunted, checking her legs for other injuries. When she reached out and touched his face, he froze. "What're you doing?" He instinctively grabbed her wrist and held her in place.

"Your face. It's bleeding."

Callum hadn't even catalogued his own injuries, only concerned with the girl. He was alive, that's all that mattered. "It's nothing, I'm sure," he said.

"Let me help." She bent over and grabbed a cottonball from the medical kit on the floor. With one hand she secured him, gently cupping his face at the jaw. With the other she blotted the wounds. "It's my fault you got hurt."

"I'm a cowboy. I've lived through much worse."

"I can see that," she said. "You have a lot of old

scars."

She began to explore his face with a fingertip, running it along the faint white lines of old injuries he remembered well. Each one told a story. The touch was new to Callum but so was the look of concern on Hailey's face. People didn't care about him. He was so used to being disregarded that he was leery of any kindness.

"Nothing to trouble yourself over."

"Are you hurt anywhere else? You had quite the scuffle."

"I said I'm fine." He stood up and backed away. Tension was making his tics act up, but this was different than before. She brought new unfamiliar feelings to the surface, ones he had no desire to explore. Whether nerves or attraction, it was best to keep his distance from the scientist and let her do her job. Love was not in the cards for a misfit like Callum.

She rose to her feet just as quickly, only reaching his chest in height. He could toss a slight thing like her over his shoulder in a heartbeat. "Take off your shirt so I can make sure. Look, it's torn and stained with blood." She snagged his shirt, making him feel more claustrophobic than ever.

Three, two, one. One, two, three. Three, two, one.

Callum brought his hand over hers. "Don't," he warned. She didn't know what she was getting into looking up at him with those big, deceptively innocent blue eyes. She'd destroy him if he allowed it. Luckily he was used to depriving himself of female companionship. It had been a long dry, fourteen months since the last time he enjoyed a woman's body. Ms. Watson wasn't going to change that now, bringing temptation to his doorstep in the guise of charity.

"Are you afraid of me?" She smiled, a slight

curve of the lips. He was just being paranoid. What was wrong with allowing her to care for his injuries? He'd just done the same for her. It meant nothing.

He tugged off his T-shirt, not wanting to appear more abnormal by refusing her offer. So far Hailey wasn't repulsed by him and his frequent subtle noises, which were quickly becoming louder and more difficult to control. He didn't want to change that now. She stared at his bare upper body for a long moment before acting. He wondered just how bad his injuries were if she was at a loss for words. Callum looked down, patting down his chest and abs. "What is it? You see something, darlin'?"

She walked around him, trailing her hand from his stomach, around his side, to his back as she moved. It was a slow, sensual drag, which had the unwelcome reaction of making his cock thicken in his jeans. "Your back," she murmured, running her fingers down his spine. "You've been a little gored yourself."

He felt perfectly fine. "You sure about that?"

"Sit. I'll clean it up," she said.

Callum sat down sideways on the chair and leaned over his knees. She rummaged through the medical kit for a minute, and then he felt the cool swipe of iodine on his broken skin. Whatever he had, it couldn't be serious. But for some reason he humored the girl, allowing her to continue touching and caring. It was addicting.

Arden never planned to marry and was quite vocal about it. He frequently told Callum that a good woman was a rarity. That their mother was the last. He supposed he'd come to believe it, not even bothering to look. If he did, it wouldn't be a girl like Hailey. She was too naïve, her skin flawless and youthful. He estimated her to be in her early twenties, young and fickle, but she claimed to be twenty-six. She wasn't even his type. He supposed the sun-kissed streaks in her dirty-blonde hair were pretty, as was her little pixie nose. *No.* He was just repressed, his dick trying to find beauty where it shouldn't.

The kitchen was like a morgue—quiet and uncomfortable. He had nothing to say, so just allowed her to finish bandaging him up.

"Where are your parents?" she finally said. The question was a simple icebreaker, but Callum never responded well when asked about his mom and dad. He bit the inside of his cheek before speaking.

"Gone," he said. "Buried back home. It's what they would have wanted."

"I'm sorry. I shouldn't have said anything."

He shrugged. Callum wanted to tell her everything. There was so much stored inside him never given a chance to be said or shared. His parents had toiled and struggled since arriving in the country decades earlier. His mother was pregnant with Arden and he came along three years later. In all the time they worked the land, they never returned to Ireland. Arden and Callum worked extra hard to save enough money to send them home for their wedding anniversary—it would be the last trip they ever made. The airport shuttle that picked them up from the airport went off the road, killing everyone instantly when it veered into oncoming traffic. The coroner said the driver went into a diabetic coma, but the cause didn't change the outcome. At least they died in their homeland, which was a small consolation to the tragedy that left two brothers alone in the world that didn't want them.

"That was a long time ago. The wounds aren't fresh." He stood up and reached around his body to feel the edge of the bandage Hailey had applied. "Am I fit to leave, nurse?"

She stared at him, a silent connection passing between them. He wondered if she felt the same thing, or if he was just so damn deprived of attention that he'd read something into nothing.

****

Hailey was at a loss for words. The man had the body of a god and had just wrestled a wild boar with his bare hands to protect her. She couldn't help that her heart pitter-pattered to a new beat, one spelling out Callum's name. Why did he remain so aloof? Did he only see her as a problem to deal with? Did she want him to look at her with lust in his eyes?

She was probably still in shock after having that wild animal trap her in the woods for so long. She'd been cold, terrified, and hopeless. At one point she'd given up, expecting never to see the light of day again. Then she heard him call her name—her savior. He was the most unlikely hero after being so abrupt with her earlier. Now she was seeing a softer side to him, although he tried to keep it under lock and key.

Callum retired to his bedroom and she settled in Arden O'Shea's old room. It felt like a presence lingered with all his personal items still on display. After slipping out of her clothes, putting on an oversized T-shirt Callum provided, she quietly padded around the room. She pulled open one of the wooden dresser drawers and found a small photo album. Hailey couldn't resist slipping it out. With only the gentle radiance of lamplight, she cuddled on the bed to look through the pictures. Most were of rodeo events with several men in the pictures. Then she came across a few of Callum and Arden. They looked a lot alike, both devastatingly handsome. What on earth could have alienated them from the rest of the town?

When she heard footsteps creaking along the

wooden floorboards outside her door, she shoved the album under the extra pillow and pulled the covers over her. The door cracked open an inch. "You still awake?" he asked.

"Come in."

The door opened fully and a nearly nude cowboy strolled in. He'd taken off his hat, shirt, and even unbuckled. His Wranglers dipped so low she could spy the masculine trail of dark hair disappearing behind his zipper. "I don't like that you didn't eat tonight. It's my place to make sure you have food. There's bread in the kitchen and I have a small vegetable plot to the side of the house. You help yourself."

"Thank you."

"You comfortable?"

"It's—It's great." She fiddled with the edge of the blanket. Part of her felt like a love struck twelve year old, shy and awkward, while another yearned for him to ravage her. It was an odd mix of desire and fear sparked by the way he stared at her. Even with the long shadows cast on the wall behind him, she could still make out the intensity in his eyes. What was he thinking?

"If you need me I'll be just down the hall."

She nodded politely, her voice not capable of working.

"And you can find me in the fields come morning." With that he slipped out the way he came, his footsteps outside the door marking his retreat. She felt bereft once he left but also exhausted from the day's events. For the first time, she fell asleep dreaming of impossible fairy tales rather than research notes.

Chapter Four

The next morning, Hailey knew she had to get started on her research as soon as possible. Callum wouldn't put up with zero progress, especially after the nightmare she'd caused yesterday. Planning out her research on paper was a lot different than implementing it in the field. She began to doubt her ability to get the job done. The wild hogs were lethal creatures if not handled properly. Studying them would be difficult in the day since they acted mostly at night. She figured lack of food in an overpopulated species was the main culprit. Finding a solution was more of a challenge. She had to come up with a long-term answer, not fall for short-term fixes like traps, shotguns, and poison suggested by many.

Once outside, she spotted Callum's combine in the fields. He wasn't too far off, so she cut through the field to reach him. The earth rumbled as the machine harvested the wheat.

"Callum!" she called out over the roar of the engine. Hailey wanted him to show her the areas being destroyed by the hogs. She'd also brought him a little picnic lunch as a peace offering.

When he still hadn't heard or noticed her, she moved ahead so he'd spot her in his line of vision. It worked because he quickly cut the engine, the motor winding down as silence once again returned to the morning.

He leapt down, adjusting his Stetson as he strode towards her. "That's a dangerous thing to do. You could have become another statistic if I hadn't spotted you."

"I brought you something," she said, changing the subject. Irritating him again hadn't been her objective. She held out the brown paper bag.

"What's this?" he asked. Callum's brow creased

as he peeked into the bag. "Food?"

"I thought you might be hungry. You've been at it since before I woke up."

"My day starts with the sun, sometimes before." He held the bag at his side, waiting for something more.

"I was going to start my research. I need to know what areas on your property the hogs are destroying."

"It's a bit out of my way right now, and I have to get this field clear before it gets too hot. Come sit for a bit."

He returned to the combine and sat on the metal running board. She noticed the small scabs forming on his face, reminding her of the night before. Hailey was tempted to run her hand over the stubble on his jaw, to use his injuries as an excuse to touch him.

"I'll have to head into town today to pick up my clothes." And everything else she owned. It would all fit in the back of her pickup. There was no sense leaving it at the boarding house another few days when she'd be forced to leave before she finished her assignment on the O'Shea Ranch. All she owned were some clothes, tons of books, and a few personal items. She chose not to put value in material items. As a child, Hailey learned that expensive toys couldn't buy love. She'd have traded everything for some quality time with her parents.

He took a bite of the apple she'd packed him, looking off into the fields he had left to clear. "I'll come with you if you can wait a couple hours. I need to pick up a few things at the market."

"Okay."

Callum finished the fruit and tossed the core. He continually cleared his throat even though they were in the middle of summer and he didn't appear sick. He was dealing with more than she could imagine. "Want to take a quick ride?" he asked, nodding to the massive machine behind him.

"I don't know…"

"Come on now. Don't be a yellow belly. After last night, I think you can handle a ride on a combine."

She reluctantly agreed, allowing him to assist her up into the mouth of the beast. There was seating for two, everything covered in a thick layer of dust. Just before she sat down, he passed a rag over the metal bench. The random kind gestures were a stark contrast to his frequent black mood swings.

Once he fired up the engine, her entire body shook. Hailey didn't know how he could stand clearing fields for hours. The machine was so noisy it was deafening, the dust and sun a constant irritant.

"Wanna drive?" he shouted.

She shook her head.

He scowled. "Don't be shy. Come here." Callum grabbed her arm and directed her to where he sat. He lowered her onto his lap, something she wasn't expecting. A rush of heat and tingles erupted once his strong arm came around her. "Hold here," he said. "Keep it straight."

"I can't."

"You're doing fine. I'm right here if you need me."

She felt like a child sitting on a grown man's lap, but the ideas swirling in her head were anything but wholesome. He leaned forward against her back, monitoring her actions. Both his arms were around her waist, one securing her to his body. Her traitorous pussy began to pulse in deep, distracting waves. This was so unlike her. Her entire life was based on her research, of finding a place to belong beyond her controlling family. She supposed she'd been trying so hard to make it on her own that she stopped caring about the woman on the inside. If she failed, proving her parents right, it would destroy not only her self-esteem but also something deeper—the sense of independence she valued.

Now, being in this cowboy's arms, feeling carefree and alive, she never wanted to return to her old way of life. It felt so good just to talk to someone about anything other than research—to be held, touched, and coddled.

She squealed when a dark cloud of black birds suddenly descended in their path. Callum only laughed, reassuring her with a kiss to the side of her neck. Her breath hitched. Had he really just kissed her? Was it a friendly peck or something more? It felt like more—like the energy of the entire world trapped into that one moment. She tried to play it off, as if it never happened. It would save her from misreading his intention.

"We'll stop when we get to the end of the row," he said, pointing ahead. When he shut down the engine once again, her unease increased. She shifted over to her own seat, not knowing what to say or do.

He leaned over and set one of his big, rough hands on her thigh. She had to stifle a gasp. "How're your knees healing?" He assessed her knees and came to his own conclusion that they needed more tending. "Not so good. I'll soak them in Epsom salt when we get back from town."

She didn't refuse him even though she knew it was unnecessary. Hailey loved the way he looked out for her, going that extra mile when he didn't have to. The vulnerable girl inside yearned for his acceptance, while the woman knew not to rush into things.

They walked the rest of the way to the house, their hands occassionally brushing. The heat was already growing in intensity. His checkered shirt was unbuttoned, and he used the corner to wipe his brow. She discreetly admired his ripped abs, surprised how just a simple look could make her body so needy.

"So, how do you plan to rid me of my hog problem, darlin'? Any ideas?"

"I–I'm not sure yet. There're a lot of variables."

"Well they've plum near destroyed all my wire fencing, and made a mess of my winter wheat crop. I hope you have some ideas."

She hoped to God she made a success of her stay. There was no way she could tell him she was clueless, only used to livestock and textbooks. These feral hogs were something new and dangerous. If she admitted that she may not even succeed, she'd never get a grant and would be homeless to boot. She had to make it work.

When they arrived at the house, Callum wanted to take a quick shower before heading into town. She fixed her hair in the dresser mirror as she waited, using Arden's comb to smooth out the knots. Hailey rarely gave much thought to her appearance. Now she cared. She wanted Callum to look at her with hunger in his eyes.

She set the comb down and stared at her reflection. *What are you doing, Hailey?* She was setting herself up for more disappointment, looking for love in the wrong places. Callum lived on his own for a reason. If he'd wanted a woman, he would have had one by now. He was wrong for her on so many levels but her attraction was undeniable.

As she made her way down the second floor hallway, Callum came out of the bathroom with a towel wrapped around his hips. His dark hair was slicked back, thin rivulets of water running down his chest. They both froze as if caught in the headlights.

"How's your back?" she asked, trying to appear unfazed by his near nudity.

"Feels fine." He hadn't moved, his voice monotone.

She took the first step, circling him until completely behind him. He ass was hard and toned under the towel, his back all defined muscle. She briefly noted the healing wound. It was minor, already scabbing over. What she really wanted was to lick the drips of water off his tanned skin. His shoulders were so broad, she craved to smooth her hands along them. Could he feel her desire? It felt like a living force all around her, tempting her to act. Hailey was a virgin, not that she'd advertise the fact. She'd rather consider herself a twenty-six year old woman at her sexual peak than inexperienced. *Touch him, just run your fingers along his back,* her inner voice demanded. But one wrong move could spell disaster if it wasn't reciprocated. Her insecurities held her back. She bit the inside of her lip hard enough to draw blood.

"Well? Am I on the mend?" he asked.

She shifted back into reality, her chance to act slipping away. "It looks good." She gently touched the marred skin. The intimate human contact was something she'd lacked and never knew it. She wanted to touch and be touched, but it had to be for the right reasons. There was no way she'd end up the town trollop being gossiped about by Cassie in the diner. Hailey wanted a relationship based on real love, not convenience or financial gain like her parents. Although most of her reading was research related, she did indulge in romance novels from time to time. If only there was a stitch of truth in the pages of those fiction books—like true, irrevocable love.

He turned his head. "I'll just be two minutes." Then he entered his room and closed the door tight. She exhaled, nearly dizzy from holding her breath. The man was so delicious, so well-built, how could she not be tempted?

****

Callum insisted they take his truck for the drive into town. It was bad enough he brought attention to himself with his Tourette's. A truck lacking a muffler was just asking for trouble. He usually liked to get what he needed and leave just as fast.

"It's the next left. The second house," she said. He knew the boarding house.

"How long have you stayed there?"

"Two years—since I finished my Masters and had to get off campus."

A boarding house wasn't a home. It didn't seem natural for a young woman to be surviving all on her own without family or a man.

"It's not much of a home," he said, pulling into the driveway.

"It's all I can afford. Just because I've spent most of my adult years in university doesn't equate a six-figure income. I'm lucky if I can buy food week to week."

"Then why bother?"

She looked at him, the sunlight reflecting off her blue eyes. "Because I love it. I love learning about people and animals, creating solutions to problems…and being independent of my family."

"Ahh, there's the heart of it, no?"

She shook her head. "Just a piece."

Hailey left the truck, trotting up the path. He lowered his window and called out. "How much you gettin'?"

"I'm taking everything," she said simply and disappeared inside the Victorian-style house. *Everything?* Did she plan to stay at his ranch that long? Permanently? He followed her into the house, needing answers. If she was clearing out, she'd also need help.

The interior was dim, forcing his eyes to adjust from the bright sunlight. He wasn't a small man, and always felt awkward around such dainty things—little antique tables with doilies, miniatures displayed on tiny shelves. If he moved the wrong way, it could be disastrous. It certainly wasn't comfortable, not a place he'd want to live in.

"Hailey?" he called out.

Old Mrs. Chambers came around the corner. "Can I help you?"

"I'm helping Ms. Watson collect her things."

"So you're the reason she's moving out? I didn't hear of a marriage proposal."

"No, ma'am. I'm just lending a hand. We ain't together in the way you're thinking." His eyes began to twitch, one worse than the other, not uncommon when he was put on the spot. It was one of the reasons he preferred his solitary lifestyle.

She huffed, lifting her chin. When Hailey peeked down from the stairs, she was his saving grace. He passed the landlady and took the stairs two at a time. Once he entered Hailey's room, she closed the door tight.

"I'm sorry. She's terrible."

"Maybe a little," he said with a smile. After a minute he realized he was standing in the middle of Hailey's room, her private domain. It was like taking a look inside the mind of the woman he knew so little about. She was neat, her bedspread made and dresser top organized. He sat heavily on the bed, enjoying the lush mattress compared to his firm one. Callum picked up one of several teddy bears and observed it. The brown bear in his hand was thread-bare from lovin'.

She tried to snatch it from him but he kept it out of her reach with an outstretched arm. "Callum!"

"What's this? Your little teddy? You best bring him along to keep you company at night."

She climbed over him until he dropped to his back, determined to retrieve her stuffed toy. "Stop it," she said, waving her arm around. He held her around the waist so she couldn't get higher. Their bodies were pressed together. It felt good having her soft curved flush to his hard muscle. She hadn't yet noticed the intimacy of their position—but she would. Was this where he wanted things to lead? Could he handle having a woman in his life full-time? It would only be a matter of time before she tired of his constant noises and physical tics—a perpetual irritation. He could scarcely stand himself some days. Since there was nothing he could do to control his body's random actions, he thought it best to avoid disappointment and stay single.

She stopped struggling, her full weight settling over his body. Her chest rose and fell in deep waves. "You're terrible," she whispered, resting the side of her face to his chest. He was surprised she felt comfortable enough to stay in such close contact. Most people feared him, or at least chose to stay away. This girl accepted him, no fear whatsoever. If only the approval could last forever.

"Just teasin'. You can keep your teddy. And we best get to work before Mrs. Chambers comes in and gives us both a spanking for being inappropriate under her roof."

"True." She rolled to her side and looked him in the eyes. Hailey reached out and cupped his face. "Thank you for being so sweet to me."

He frowned. "I did what any other man would have done," he assured. Callum didn't think he'd done anything extraordinary. Certainly nothing to earn him such attention.

"No, you're special."

She slipped off the bed and pulled out a couple of empty suitcases from the closet, ending the moment that made time stand still for Callum.

He sat up. "Everything's going? Including these?" He held up the bears.

"Yes, everything, Callum." The sound of his name on her lips was the sweetest thing. It seemed every hour he spent with Hailey increased her beauty in his eyes. She was no longer the annoying girl from the university. She'd transformed, and now he swore he looked at an angel as she hurried to fill the bags with her folded clothing. Her long blonde hair fell to the side like a silken fan, her feminine fingers moving ever so daintily to fold and organize.

Together, they emptied all the drawers and shelves. When he got to her bottom drawer, the ache in his balls increased. All her intimate wear was organized into the one place—lace and cotton panties and brassieres of every color. He couldn't help but imagine her wearing the little bits. The fact she kept well covered left his imagination on overdrive. When he held up a whisper thin piece of black lace, she grabbed it away.

"Hey!"

"What? I'm helping."

She used both arms to scoop out all the drawer's contents at once, shoving it into a shopping bag. After half an hour the room was cleared out and loaded into Callum's truck. They were ready to head off to the market. He needed to get more food than usual to accommodate Hailey and her special diet. Steak and chicken were the main staples after potatoes and corn, but she wouldn't touch them.

They drove to the market, the sun now high in the sky. He left his shirt in the truck, only wearing his black tank top. Even so, he still felt like he was walking in a sauna. "It's a scorcher," he said.

"And you don't have air-conditioning at your place, do you?"

"Just the river cutting through the west end of the property, and perhaps some shade from the weeping willows out back."

"I guess that'll have to do."

Walking side by side, they checked out all the fresh produce being sold at the market. He felt an odd possessiveness about Hailey, which he had no right feeling. She wasn't his and he had no plans on changing that. She squeezed some fruits, knocked on others, and smelled the rest. It was amusing watching her choose what to buy. When he'd come alone, he'd grab what he needed and be gone in the blink of an eye.

"What do you think?" Hailey approached him with a watermelon in her arms. He took her load, weighing it in his palms. "Do you like watermelon?" she asked.

It was one of his favorites, a rare treat. "There ain't much I won't eat."

"We can have it tonight after dinner. This one has to be sweet."

He chuckled. "It's passed all your tests, has it?"

His carefree mood was spoiled when he spotted one of the objects of his angst. Jeremy Majors and two of his lackeys entered the market. Normally he wouldn't care about dealing with them. He was used to their verbal abuse and was man enough to handle anything else they wanted to dish out. But he was with Hailey. The thought of being humiliated in front of her brought his nerves rushing to the surface. His Tourette's immediately flared, embarrassing guttural sounds escaping from his lips in a rapid sequence. He felt like a spectacle, unable to stop the train wreck he was becoming.

"What's the matter?" she asked, a look of concern on her face.

"Nothing. We should go, though." His eyes must have been zeroed in on Jeremy's approach because she turned around to see.

"Look, the retard has a girlfriend."

Chapter Five

Hailey was brushed aside as Callum barreled forward. He grabbed the other man by the collar, nearly bringing him off his feet. Callum was bigger than most men she'd ever met, tall and built. For another man to goad him was a fool's cry for attention.

One of the guy's friends hit Callum from the side, which only appeared to aggravate him more. He tossed the man he held to the ground and threw a solid punch to the gut of the other. His enemy crashed into one of the fruit displays, apples spilling out in every direction. Shoppers created a wide arch of space around the melee, careful not get too close to Callum. He looked like a born fighter, every muscle taut and defined.

Her only concern was that he didn't get hurt.

"You no-good, piece of shit," called the first guy, picking up a broken, wooden table leg as a weapon.

"Callum!" she yelled.

He turned around just in time to grab the club before it struck him. She hadn't noticed at first but there were three guys against Callum. As he wrestled the weapon from one, another came up from behind and sucker punched him several times in the side. He was weakening, the sight terrifying her. Nobody else would step in to help even though the fight was three to one. She screamed as they ganged up on the lone cowboy. She felt desperate, unable to help.

Just as one of attackers got the wooden table leg free, raising it to strike Callum in the head, a stranger grabbed it in a strong fist.

"What the fuck?" The man turned around, coming face to face with the cowboy she only knew from pictures. "Ar–Arden O'Shea?" He grabbed the collar of his friend, all three looking like they'd seen the angel of death. They ran off, not looking back. She'd never seen grown men become so afraid by the presence of one solitary man. Was Arden's reputation that severe?

Callum was still on the ground. She was about to run over to him when Arden blocked her way. He tilted her chin up so she was forced to look at him square in the eyes. He looked strikingly similar to Callum, the same height and broadness, but his hair was unruly and eyes as blue as the mid-day sky. "You best take my little brother home." It was all he said, his Irish accent working magic on her libido. Then he strode off, people clearing a path for him. He had a strong air of confidence, as if he owned the ground he walked on.

Was he home for good? Callum said he hadn't seen him in a year. Would he take back his room now? If so, what would become of her now that she'd given up her place at the boarding house? The landlady said she had a waiting list, so getting it back was an impossibility—not that she had money without a new grant.

She watched Arden depart, his spurs chiming as he walked, then turned and ran over to Callum. He was already dusting himself off with his Stetson, no worse for wear. "Are you okay?" she asked, patting him down for injuries.

"I'm fine," he said curtly. "Where's that watermelon of yours?"

She pointed to the ground. It was still in once piece. Callum bent over and picked it up, bringing it to the cash out. The lady took his money without a word, everyone staring as they returned to the truck.

He started up the engine and drove in complete silence, looking straight at the road ahead. She felt a twisted knot in her gut, a mix of unease, pity, and insecurity.

"Who was that guy? Did you know him?"

"Jeremy Majors. We went to school together."

The truck jostled as he handled the dirt roads with less caution than necessary. She didn't say anything else. He was likely pissed off and embarrassed. Hailey wouldn't even try to imagine what it was like to live in his shoes. Once back at the O'Shea Ranch, Callum took off, slamming the truck door, and disappeared into the barn. She didn't know if she should go after him or give him time to cool off. She'd never known someone so passionate, both tender and volatile all rolled into one.

It was probably the worst choice, but she followed him.

"Callum?" she whispered. The inside of the barn was dim. It smelled strong of hay dust, oats, and leather. There was a creak in the wooden floorboards above her, some dust raining down on her, so she knew he was up in the loft. Hailey climbed the rickety ladder and found him standing at the open loft doors, staring out into the fields. The sun was lowering on the horizon, not yet set.

"You shouldn't be up here," he said without turning around.

"I'm worried about you."

"Why?"

"You could have been hurt. Were you hurt?"

"I'm not a fucking child," he snapped. "I said I'm fine."

She felt slightly apprehensive. Was he capable of hurting a woman? Did she know him enough to feel completely safe?

"Obviously you're not. It can help to talk things out." His random noises were increasing, along with the throat clearing. The harsh sounds stole the peaceful calm of twilight—but she didn't blame him. Instead, she felt drawn to the mysterious cowboy, desperate to help his plight in any way she could.

He whirled around, fire in his eyes. "If I liked to talk I wouldn't be living out here alone, now would I? Everything was just fine until *you* showed up. And I'm no better off than before you came, the hogs still running amuck."

She took a cleansing breath, reminding herself he was speaking out of anger. Her years of studies flooded her mind. He was reacting to the unjust treatment, and Tourette's was known to flare up in times of undue stress. Still, she wouldn't encourage him to alienate her. "You know what? I thought you were a nice guy, but maybe I was wrong."

"Damn straight you were wrong. I'm on the town's most unwanted list, or didn't you check before taking the job? It was only a matter of time until you discovered what kind of a freak I was anyway."

"What kind of freak would that be, Callum?" Her patience was wearing thin. His self-abuse was unhealthy and unnecessary. "You can stop trying to scare me off because it won't work."

"Are you that hard up for a room that you'd put up with the likes of me?"

"Stop it," she warned. "I'm here because I want to be."

"Well ain't that just dandy. I'll stay out of your way until you get your research done. No reason we need to deal with each other." He walked by her to leave, but she grabbed his arm. His muscles were tense, his bicep too large to hold securely.

"Stop being such an asshole!"

He froze for a moment, and she wondered if she'd made a huge mistake, pushing him too far. If he hit her, she'd survive. She braced for the worst, closing her eyes as time stood still.

She wouldn't be able to stop him should he decide to leave. He would dictate the next step. When he wrapped a hand around both her upper arms, walking her backwards, she opened her eyes in a flash. He pressed her flat to the wooden slat wall, holding her firmly in place so she couldn't move. "I'm a monster, Hailey. Look at me for what I am, dammit. You must be blind not to see what the townsfolk see." He leaned in and inhaled at her neckline. Her pussy moistened.

"I see a man choosing to hide away from society rather than face his problems head-on. Stop feeling sorry for yourself."

He stared at her as if seeing her for the first time. His eyes narrowed, his hands tightening around her arms. "You don't know what you're talkin' about. And you're playing with fire, little one. Maybe I should give you a sample of why society chooses to keep away." There was a hint of threat in his tone, but he didn't scare her. Not any more. He may not know it, but he was testing her, trying to find loyalty or betrayal. Hailey lived for this, lived for the challenge of understanding the mind. Callum's was both highly complex and simple at the same time.

"Go ahead," she dared.

His jaw clenched down hard, his dark eyes boring into hers. "Dangerous games you like to play." Callum hoisted her up over his shoulder, stealing her air, and carried her to the far end of the hay loft where shadows dominated. He dropped her down on some open flakes, straddling her legs and pinning her arms to the sides.

"What are you going to do to me?"

His eyes cleared for a moment. "Don't flatter yourself, little girl," he said. "When my daddy was alive, do you know what he did when we misbehaved? He gave us the belt." He used one hand to secure her wrists above her head and used the other to slide his thick leather belt from his Wranglers.

"You wouldn't dare!"

"You think there's something good in me? You're wrong. And I'm about to prove that."

Her heart raced as he made a loop with the belt. She'd never been spanked in her life, but she'd always been an obedient child. He fought to unbutton her jeans and she struggled to stop him. Once unfastened, he attempted to roll her to her belly. No way would she willingly let him hide her ass.

"Stop, Callum!" She was exhausted, near tears from frustration. His burst of energy appeared to quickly diminish after she said his name, his movements sluggish. She could feel some of his weight over her, the heat of his breath against her neck, and his fingers interlocked with hers.

"You should leave," he whispered.

"No."

He growled, an exasperated sound of a man pushed to the edge. His hand travelled from her hand, up her arm, until he reached the side of her neck. He stroked her skin with his thumb. "I'm a monster," he reminded.

"You're not."

When he dropped his head again, she kissed his neck as he'd done to her in the morning. It felt right. It also unleashed a floodgate of desire she didn't realize resided inside her. She continued to kiss him, nudging his face with hers, needing more. The passionate release of emotion, combined with their physical exertion, created a ripe atmosphere to explore their desires.

"Hailey..." He relaxed his grip on her. She immediately began to touch his body, having craved to feel his muscles every time she saw him. He was hard and toned, all male. She slid one hand under his tank top, skin to skin.

"Kiss me," she begged. The air snapped with erotic tension. If he chose to fuck her right there in the hay, she'd welcome it. Her body felt like a furnace, liquid heat threatening to escape any minute.

When he turned his face to hers, she licked the seam of his lips, but he didn't give her access. Why was he so reluctant? Was she alone in her desires? Had she pegged him wrong all along and he really did hate her?

His breathing was heavier but he still refused to act, finally pulling off her body and standing. "Trust me. You don't want a man like me." Then he climbed down the stairs leaving her achy and wanting.

****

Refusing Hailey had been the hardest thing in the world for Callum to do. His cock was painfully hard, every cell in his body screaming within him to take her, to drown in her heat. Her pink lips were full and tempting. He wanted to feel them brush against his, to know her entire body intimately.

When she had first shown up, he didn't even bat an eye. After only two days he'd already developed a physical attraction to the girl. His fondness continued to grow, a dangerous prospect for Callum. Men like him didn't have families. They survived on the fringe of society.

He'd been humiliated at the market, ousted for his differences, brought down several pegs in front of the only girl that mattered. She'd looked at him like a regular man, treated him normally even when his Tourette's got out of hand. It had been a dream all along. Jeremy's attack only proved a relationship would never work. He was ashamed of who he was and would never be accepted by others, no matter how much he wanted to fit in. Hailey deserved a normal life with a normal man. He had a dark history, one filled with painful memories beginning when he was just a young boy. One girl couldn't undo decades of damage with sweet words and promises of sex. He was a lost cause.

He kicked off his boots after entering the kitchen. His symptoms were driving him nuts, always acting up at the most inopportune times. Some days he'd scream as loud as he could out in the fields, other times he'd punch a wall so hard his knuckles would bleed. It was all in vain. His Tourette's had no cure, no magic pill, and nothing he did would ease the symptoms. His curse, one passed down from generation to generation of O'Shea men, was his whether he deserved it or not. Arden had been lucky to escape unscathed, as normal as any other person. But he squandered the gift of normalcy Callum yearned for, drinking his life away.

Callum crashed onto his bed, hot, bothered, and angry with the world. He was used to Jeremy and all the other assholes who felt they had the right to bring him down. He'd learned to ignore them. Hailey was the problem. In only a couple days she'd given him hope, made him dream of a life that was never meant for him. He was better off before she showed up on his doorstep.

He combed his hands through his hair, staring at the ceiling. What if it took Hailey a month to conduct her research? He had to avoid her at all costs. She was confused, pumped up on the adrenaline from the earlier chaos. But once the dust settled she'd realize what a loser he was, and what a mistake it would be to invest in him. He may be a fuck-up, but he wouldn't take advantage of a woman's trust.

Chapter Six

For the rest of the week Hailey found fresh fruit and vegetables on the kitchen counter every morning. She never saw Callum. He left the house before the sun rose and he avoided her at every cost. She'd thought things were just starting to go well between them…now she didn't know what to think. She had to return to treating the assignment as the research it was. Daydreams and fantasies about the Irish cowboy would only serve to dampen her spirits.

She'd made minor progress in tracking the hogs' lifestyle, their eating and sleeping habits, and preferred diet. She was testing sound deterrents, natural scents, and other known wildlife inhibitors.

Hailey was boiling some pasta late one afternoon when the screen door whacked shut. She jumped, turning around in a hurry, nearly knocking over the pot.

"Why didn't you tell me you saw Arden at the market?" Callum's voice was deep and irate. His accent was always more defined when he was mad. This was the first time he'd acknowledged her existence in days, and even though the attention was negative, she was glad to hear his voice. She didn't know how he handled the loneliness for a year alone.

"You haven't exactly spoken with me since."

He paced the kitchen until the door opened again. "That's not the homecoming I was expecting," said Arden. He watched Hailey from across the room and it felt as if he undressed her with those narrowed blue eyes.

"You left! What right do you have to waltz back in after a year on the road?" asked Callum.

Arden was the opposite of his brother—calm, controlled, and confident. "I believe it's my name on the deed, little brother. Now stop being such a baby and welcome me home proper."

"I won't. I've been busting my balls on this ranch since you left. Not even a damned phone call from you."

They faced off as if she wasn't in the room. She felt like an outsider looking in.

"You think I want to live like this, preserving a relic from the past? I want more from my life than horse shit and lonely nights. You're the one dead set in not selling, and throwing your life away," said Arden.

"If your ideas were so great, then why are you back? Shouldn't you be living the high life in the city, sipping margaritas with your classy friends?"

"What? I can't miss my kid brother?" Arden pulled out a wooden chair and sat down, leaning over his knees. "You know I've worried about you every day. And as soon as I get into town I find the same assholes trying to pick a fight with you. This town has nothing for us, Callum."

"It's our home. Mom and Dad built everything on this ranch. How could you sell something that's priceless?"

"It's time to move on. I can't fight for you forever."

"We're not in grade school anymore, Arden. You don't have to beat down every jerk who tries to mock me. I can handle it. I *have* been handling it."

Arden grumbled his disagreement. Once they'd both been silent for a few minutes, quietly contemplating, they seemed to remember she was in the room with them at the same moment.

"That's right… I heard you were keeping a cute young thing with you on the ranch, but I didn't believe it until I saw her at the market with my own eyes." Arden stood up, his leather boots creaking. He approached her, taking measured steps as if she were a skittish green broke horse.

"She's not mine. She does research for the university."

"An educated woman," said Arden, his gaze taking in every detail of her face. She swallowed hard.

"I'm–I'm trying to help with the hogs." She bit her lip to keep from talking. The man exuded raw sexuality, it was hard not to become affected.

"It's dinner hour. That mean you're staying on?"

She nodded.

"And where would you be sleeping?" He stared at her like a hawk. He knew she was staying in his bed, it was written all over his face. Her senses became magnified—the sound of the boiling water behind her, the shift in Callum's stance, and the barn door flapping in the distance. Could Arden feel her anxiousness, her desire?

There was something magical about this place, these two men. Her life at the university was another realm where she was a different person, a nameless face where she had to fight to be noticed. She felt more alive here, living simply, at one with nature. The desperate need to advance, to prove herself, didn't overpower her thoughts on the O'Shea Ranch. She was discovering herself after a lifetime of studying and stifling her emotions. It was more important for her to learn about Callum, and to earn back his favor. Unraveling a complex man was more engaging than learning about wild hogs.

"*Your* room," she whispered in reply. He wasn't reluctant to invade her personal space. A faint scent of alcohol and musk clung to him. He reminded her of the great outdoors, untamed and free.

"Now that'll be a problem."

"Leave her alone," said Callum. "You've been in

town for nearly a week, so you've obviously been staying somewhere. Maybe you should go there now."

****

Arden had perfected the ability to control his temper over the years. He had hot blood from his father running through his veins. It wasn't easy to rile him but mess with his family and he couldn't hold back. Fighting came natural to him. It got him kicked out of high school more times than he could count, and he had the scars to prove it. The O'Shea reputation started with their father not taking shit when local distributors tried to rip him off by paying less per ton than other non-Irish farmers. It carried on when Arden refused to let the school boys tease his brother.

Callum meant the world to him. He was the reason he'd stayed on the family ranch for so long. He felt a duty to be his little brother's protector, to maintain that one familial link left in his life.

He'd tried to leave, but he found drifting to not be all he expected. He was thirty-two now and the cowboys he competed against in the rodeo were twenty-year olds in the prime of their career. He couldn't compete with that. He found he spent more time in local pubs trying to forget absolutely everything—his parents, his brother, his career…his loneliness.

He could tell Callum had a thing for the little blonde. She was cute, an air of innocence surrounding her. He usually went for confident women, experienced in pleasuring a man. He wasn't below paying for sex, either. It was simpler that way—no emotional bother. But since the girl was staying in his bed, she was fair game.

"Maybe I'll just have to share a bed with… What's your name, sweet thing?"

"Hailey Watson."

"Pretty." He ran the backs of his fingers along her jaw, watching her quickly fall for his charms. It was so easy. Then Callum's heavy hand came down on his shoulder, forcing him to turn around.

"There's plenty of good hay in the barn."

Maybe little brother liked Ms. Watson more than he expected. He'd never seen Callum act so possessively. He usually drifted through life, trying to steer clear from everyone. The fact he let someone stay on the ranch was shocking.

"No, I've come a long way to enjoy my own bed," said Arden. "I've been dreaming about it all those nights on the road."

"Then she'll stay with me."

Hailey looked up, locking eyes with Callum. So, she felt something for his brother in return. He'd always hoped Callum would be able to find a woman of his own one day, a good woman, one who'd love him unconditionally. But he gave up hope long ago. It was increasingly evident that people with Tourette's were the brunt of every cruel and crude joke. It wasn't just the townsfolk. The uneducated slurs were on the big screen, local television, and popular radio stations. There was no escape for his brother.

He shrugged. "Whatever suits you, Callum. I have to head back into town to pick up a few things. Be back in a few hours." It was time to goad Callum, to bring some sibling rivalry into the mix. He had to keep from laughing when he lifted Hailey's hand and kissed her knuckles. "Until we meet again, baby doll."

Callum grabbed him by the sleeve and damn near threw him out of the kitchen, slamming the door behind him. He chuckled as he walked to his truck, pulling a small flask from his inside pocket. Being back on the old ranch brought him mixed feelings. Although there was a sense of security in the familiarity, he also experienced an overshadowing feeling of doom and gloom. He didn't want to live out the rest of his life isolated from the world, no chance of a future. His daddy came to their country, worked like a dog, and died just as broke and weary as when he started. Arden wanted more—he just didn't know what, yet.

****

Bastard, bastard, bastard! Arden showed up out of the blue and immediately went after his woman. Well, not his woman, but Arden didn't know that. He may be the little brother, but only by three years, and he was no smaller in size. Powerful surges of jealousy nearly made him dizzy. His fucking Tourette's was testing him, pushing him over the edge, as if things weren't bad enough between him and Hailey.

He felt like an ass, but that's what he'd wanted—to push her away. Now he wasn't so sure.

"Do you know what a charmer is?" he asked, his breathing still labored. Callum closed the distance between them.

"I suppose."

"That's what my brother is. He'll use you, get what he wants, and then be gone faster than the morning dew in summer."

She scoffed. "Did I appear to fall for sweet words and kisses?"

"Most women do when it comes to Arden."

She turned around and stirred her pasta. "Not me."

Why couldn't words come to him as easily as Arden? He'd never be able to woo a woman properly, even if he wanted to.

"Then you're a rarity." He turned to leave. "I'll be in the yard."

"Callum!"

He stopped dead, closing his eyes and taking a breath out of her sight. With his back still to her, he replied, "What is it?"

"Why are you mad at me?" There was insecurity in her tone, a pleading note. He wanted to wipe it away when he was the one to put it there in the first place.

"I ain't mad at you or anyone. I'm just tired is all."

"Of what?"

"Life."

She ran both her palms down his back. He stiffened, straightening his posture. Callum hadn't expected her to touch him or reach out after the way he'd treated her. Was it a sign?

"Don't say that. Life is whatever you make it." She nudged him until he turned. Those beautiful, big, doe eyes looked up at him. He was immediately held captive.

"Only I don't have a full deck. You saw for yourself how others look at me. I guarantee they'd look at you the same way if we were an item."

"I guess it's good I don't care then." She smiled. He'd missed that sweet smile, and felt like an asshole for trying to steal it away.

"You say that now…"

The boiling water began to make the pot lid dance. She rushed over and turned off the stove. She mustn't have expected to see him because she was only wearing a skimpy pair of cotton shorts and a tank top which barely covered her midriff. She had a fine figure. As she reached over the stove, he caught a glimpse of her panties. White.

His control wavered. What would it feel like to spend a night with a woman who meant more to him than just cheap thrills? It was a recipe for disaster, one his heart probably wouldn't survive should things go sour. But he couldn't keep away. Her soft little body called to him, a beacon in a stormy sea.

He wrapped his arms loosely around her waist from behind, savoring the feel of having her close. He'd been lying to himself. Callum did want to own her, to call her *his* woman. But the commitment and potential for disaster terrified him.

Her breath hitched. Hailey spun around in his arms.

"You're staying in my room tonight," he said.

She nodded.

"Nothing will happen unless you want it to happen," he reassured.

"I want it," she murmured, lips swollen and delectable. Hailey fiddled with the buttons on his shirt, seeming to completely forget about her meal. "You know I want it."

He still remembered the day he'd left her in the hayloft rather than making love to her. It had been a mistake, but he was too emotionally compromised at the time.

"I don't know about the boys at the university, but things may be different than you're used to."

"Such as?"

He smirked. "Bigger and better for one. And a little rough."

"Doesn't sound too scary."

His cock thickened by the second. She had no idea the restraint he was using. If he let go, he'd probably take her right on the kitchen floor. "Not scary at all." He pulled her against his erection and leaned down to kiss her neck. The sweet scent of her shampoo drove him wild like an aphrodisiac to an already aroused male. He wouldn't be able to wait until he got her in his bed. She was so warm, so ripe, so *his*.

"That feels good," she said, wriggling against his cock.

He lifted her up under the arms and set her on the counter. They were more equal in height now since she was so tiny in comparison. She wrapped her legs around his hips, spurring him to keep going. His resolve to keep professional diminished, his libido taking control.

Callum slid his hands under her shirt, cupping her bare breasts. They were soft and perfect, filling his hands nicely. "It's been a long time for me," he confessed. "You're so…so soft."

"Your hands are rough. I like it." Her willingness to accept him despite his distracting syndrome made him want her even more. He felt accepted, understood.

"I may just break a slight thing like you."

She smoothed her hands over the expanse of his shoulders. "I wonder how that would feel."

He wanted to show her. Callum stepped back a foot and tugged off his shirt. She watched him with fascination in her eyes. He unbuckled his leather belt and brought down his zipper, groaning once he had more space for his ever-growing cock. Still sheathed by his boxers, he moved on to Hailey.

"Arms up," he said.

She complied without complaint, raising her arms so he could remove her shirt. Her breasts were beautiful, youthful, sloping out into tempting peaks. Too tempting not to sample. He wrapped his arms around her hips and buried his face in her lush tits. When he sucked a firm nipple into his mouth, she let out a strangled moan, signaling her readiness to be fucked.

"Brace the counter. These are coming off," he said, hooking his fingers around the waistband of her shorts. He slid off her panties at the same time, leaving her completely nude on his kitchen counter. Callum took a cleansing breath, the red hue from the sunset flooding the kitchen in a warm bath of light. She was the ultimate temptation, a siren he couldn't ignore.

She reached for him, a wanton glaze in her eyes. "Kiss me."

"If I start, I won't be able to stop. Do you have anything against doing this here?"

"Do you?"

He kissed her hard on the lips. He'd been wanting to kiss her since that first day. The reality wasn't disappointing. Callum lost himself in her taste, the heat of her breasts against his chest, and her probing hands testing his muscles. As he gave himself over to his passion, his tics eased, leaving him in rare peace. He pulled her tight to his body, carrying her to the kitchen table, not breaking their kiss. Her tongue was lively, keeping him on his toes.

The table was solid oak, built by his daddy before he was born. If anything could support Hailey as he rode her hard, it would be the kitchen table.

"You look good enough to eat," he said, spreading her legs at the knees. Her blonde hair pooled on the wood as she watched his every move. Her pussy was glistening from an overflow of moisture, so pink and swollen. He'd love to feast on her, to rub his face in her folds as he made her scream for release. But he was in no shape to deny himself tonight.

"Come to me," she said, reaching out. He didn't deny her, dropping over her and feasting on her tits. He fiddled with his boxers, freeing his cock.

"Oh, baby, you drive me crazy. I have to have you." He ran the head of his cock along her slick folds, preparing himself.

"Then take me," she said.

Callum positioned his body securely between her legs, aiming his erection at his target. As he slid into her pussy, he thought the tightness would be his end. "Fuck, you're tight, darlin'."

He was only a couple inches in when she sprung her news on him. "I'm a virgin."

Callum froze, his cock pulsing in her cunt, eager to continue. "No, you're not. You're twenty-six."

"You're my first."

"Well, it's too late to stop now, Hailey. Do you want me to stop?" *Please say no.*

She touched his face. "I want you to be my first. I'm not afraid. Not with you."

Knowing he was her first made him feel even more possessive. He also wanted to be her last. He was the only man to know her sweet, little body—she was his. Now he faced a difficult dilemma. He'd never been harder or hornier, but he had to take her virginity tenderly like any good man would.

"Tell me if I hurt you." He eased in, inch by inch, his eyes lolling back in his head. Callum intertwined his fingers with hers at the sides of her head. He kissed her temple, then her lips—soft, individual kisses. They were promises. He'd always be there for her. He'd never hurt her. Callum hoped she could feel his intentions because he'd never been good with flowery words.

Chapter Seven

Hailey accepted Callum into her body, welcoming him. It was more than sex, it was a bond, a cementing of a new relationship. She'd known there was something between them before he started giving her the cold shoulder. The past week had been difficult for her. Lonely. She missed talking with him, saddened that their budding connection was stifled so soon. She could scarcely focus on her research when he dominated her thoughts. Now she had an abundance of hope. Or was it just sex for Callum, a momentary bout of passion?

Right now Hailey only focused on his cock filling her to the hilt. He was thick and long, her walls stretched to the max. The groans he made were masculine music to her ears. She wanted him to enjoy himself, to never forget his pleasure came from her body. Although she'd waited twenty-six years to lose her dreaded virginity, she was glad she'd waited. It made all the difference sharing it with a man she could imagine forever with, a man she respected.

"You okay?" he asked.

He'd gone so slow, something she didn't think he was capable of. She'd prepared herself for a hard, unforgiving fuck. Her body was ready, moist, and anxious. But he was a tender, patient lover. He continued to amaze her.

"You can't hurt me. I feel—I feel like I'm burning inside. Only you can make it better." It was the best way to describe the inferno building in her cunt. Her toes curled as the energy spread outwards. She wanted him to fuck her, to work his cock inside her until she screamed his name.

"Yes, ma'am." He pulled back and thrust back in, over and over. The rhythm slowly increased in speed and strength. He slid both of his forearms under her shoulders, securing her to his body. She kissed his lightly stubbled jawline, seeking his lips.

"More," she said.

Her word was the final catalyst. Callum fucked her so hard the heavy oak table screeched against the hardwood floor. She kept her legs around his hips, anchoring herself to his body. Pulsing waves began to roll through her, warning of an impending orgasm. It felt heavenly, a bliss she wanted to live in forever. Each thrust of his hips brought her closer to a precipice, his pubic bone rubbing deliciously against her clit with each upstroke.

"Oh God, Callum!"

"Come on, now. Let me feel you squeeze my cock. Claim me like I'm about to claim you." He drove into her like a finely tuned machine, his sweat-slick body a beautiful sight with the gentle cast of twilight from the window highlighting all his flexing muscles.

He seemed to know how to help her along, grinding against her and tweaking her nipple. His pace was furious, making her cry out and beg for him to make her come. It was exquisite torture.

When she finally detonated, the world stopped for those precious seconds. It felt as if she soared high above their bodies on a cloud, the wash of satisfaction incomparable. Then she fell down hard, her body contracting in violent waves as her pussy milked Callum's cock. It was an orgasm beyond her wildest expectations.

He grunted and groaned, squeezing the air out of her as he held her tight, releasing inside her body. She'd done it, kissed her virginity good-bye. Hailey had expected her future to consist of late nights reading research books, a half dozen cats lounging around her.

No longer. She had the chance at a real life, a happily ever after she never expected to achieve.

When all was said and done, the lust settled, Callum didn't disappear as he usually did. He carefully scooped her up into his strong arms, carrying her up the old staircase to his bedroom. She'd never been in his room. He always kept the door shut and she dare not peek and invade his privacy.

It was dark inside, the heavy curtains pulled shut. He kicked the door closed behind him and then walked her across the room.

"I'm actually glad Arden showed up. If it weren't for him, I'd never have had the nerve to talk to you again." He settled her down on his bed. The mattress was firm and the bedding smelled like him, all male.

"I've missed you. I'm not good with the silent treatment." Her sterile childhood was nothing to covet. All she wanted from Callum was warmth and acceptance. He climbed in bed beside her, pulling a heavy comforter over their bodies. Callum spooned her from behind, tucking her in close. He kissed her shoulder, and she felt utterly wanted.

"I didn't mean to hurt you...well, maybe I did at first. This is all new to me, but I'm going to try my best not to sabotage things between us."

"Is there an *us*?" she whispered.

He ran the backs of his fingers up and down her arm, his breath warm on the back of her neck. "A farmer doesn't rush his harvest."

"What does that mean?"

"It means we have to take things a day at a time and see where they lead."

She'd just given Callum her virginity, her heart, her everything. The new path her life was suddenly taking was exciting and she wanted to jump in with both feet. But, of course, he was right. Rushing a commitment was bound to sour any relationship.

"That's fair," she said.

"You sound disappointed."

She shrugged. "I've just been on my own for so long. It will be nice to finally belong somewhere."

"Don't be frettin'. You're mine now. I just have to get used to having a woman around."

They fell asleep in each other's arms. By the time she opened her eyes the next morning, a sliver of light peeking in through the curtain, Callum was gone. She sighed contentedly, rolling to her back. Her body was deliciously sore. Her cowboy would be out harvesting one of his fields. She wondered if Arden even returned home last night and if he'd start helping Callum around the farm. God knows he needed the respite. All she could do was focus on ridding the property of pesky hogs, which would hopefully make his life easier.

****

When the weekend came around, Arden decided it was time to have a word with Callum's guest. He could see love in his brother's eyes, and he wouldn't have her break his heart. Just like when they were kids, his need to look out for Callum was strong.

She was sitting in the long grass behind the house with a couple of textbooks that looked heavier than her. The wind gently picked up the ends of her blonde hair, her feminine scent travelling all the way to where he stood.

He approached her. "Something interesting?" he asked.

Hailey looked up at him, the sun reflecting in her blue eyes. "Oh...just some research. I think I'm finally onto something."

"That's good. I hear it's been two weeks already.

How long you plan on staying?"

"I–I haven't thought about it. These things take time."

He walked around the area, alternately taking in the views and watching her reactions. "You know my brother ain't simple, if that's what you're thinking. He's smarter than I am. You can't believe the calculations he can do in his head."

"I never thought that."

"You sure? Most people do." Arden was skeptical of everyone, especially cute little blondes capable of destroying his brother.

She closed her textbook. "Look, I know he has Tourette's Syndrome."

"He tell you?"

"It's obvious, and I did a thesis on it in my second year of studies, among other neurological disorders."

He rubbed his chin, trying to figure her out. What was her deal? Surely she didn't want Callum for a relationship. She could get any man of her choosing, educated men who could take proper care of her. "So you know it has no cure?"

"And I also know it has no impact on intelligence, and the tics are completely involuntary."

"Fancy talk."

"Meaning it's not his fault. I would never judge a man for something he was born with. And the disorder is more common than you think, just not as severe as Callum's."

He crouched down beside her, taking a lock of her hair between his fingers. "And what's your story, Ms. Watson?"

She looked at him shyly, as if uncomfortable with his closeness. "I've been trying to make something of my career for the past two years but so far nothing seems to be panning out."

"Before that?"

"Six years of university."

"Just the thought of that makes my head hurt. What makes a person dedicate that much of their lives to the almighty dollar?"

"It wasn't about money for me. My parents are both doctors and expected me to follow in their footsteps. When I didn't specialize in family medicine, they disowned me. I've been on my own ever since."

"You haven't seen them in all these years?"

She shook her head.

Arden couldn't understand some families. His parents were deceased, but when they were alive he'd do anything for them. Even now, he'd die for his only sibling, Callum. Blood ties were supposed to stick together through any trial or tribulation. This girl had healthy parents, apparently well-to-do. It seemed a sin to stay apart over matters of money and career choices. One day it would be too late to make amends. Personally, he couldn't live with that kind of guilt, which was part of the reason he decided to return home to the O'Shea Ranch. Even the isolation and fruitless outlook of life on the farm weren't as bad as estranging his brother.

"So what happens to you now?" He dropped down to his side, supporting himself on an elbow. The sun was strong, set in a clear sky. "You volunteer your time to different ranches in exchange for room and board?"

"I need more research before the university will consider giving me another grant."

"So this isn't about helping Callum?"

"It is. I'm helping him while helping myself. There's nothing wrong with that, is there?"

"There is if he's falling in love with you."

She froze, her lips parting. "Did he say that?"

"I haven't spoken more than two words to him since arriving. I think my little brother is working hard at avoiding me."

Hailey began to stack her books, readying to leave. He reached out and snagged her wrist, keeping her on the grass with him.

"Maybe you should be more supportive now that you're back," she said boldly.

He smirked. "So you have a little fire inside you after all."

"No, I just care about Callum. It's not natural for one man to tend all this land on his own."

The property was huge, but their daddy had managed on his own until they were old enough to do their part. Hard work never killed a man. It was laziness that was the root to many evils.

He took out his flask, feeling the urge for a quick drink. Her eyes narrowed as he tilted the silver flask against his lips. "What is it?" he asked, pausing.

"What's in that? Alcohol?"

"Want some?"

She pulled back slightly. "I don't drink. And neither should you if all the stories are true."

"There're lots of stories chasing around. If you were the smart girl you say you are, you wouldn't listen to gossip and hearsay."

"Then what's the truth? *Are* you a no-good Irish drunkard?"

He cocked an eyebrow. "That's what they're saying?" Arden nearly choked on his own spit. That must have been the funniest thing he'd heard in a long while.

"One of many things."

"Did you hear any stories about how I'm such an

excellent lover?"

Her cheeks flushed.

"No? Then how about I show you? Then you can spread your own firsthand gossip."

"I have to go." She tugged her arm away.

"Wait, wait…" He tucked his flask out of sight. "Forgive me, darlin'. I'm slow to trust, especially after being on the road for nearly a year."

"I'm not usually one to listen to gossip, but you haven't exactly made a good case for yourself so far."

He got to his feet, brushing the dry grass from his black Wranglers. "Let me change that then. How about I take you for a ride?"

"I have research to finish."

"It won't take long. It's good to let loose once in a while." He wanted to see how much effort it took to get Hailey to smile, and how long it would take for her to agree to bed him. Arden's life was simple. His few pleasures were a good fight, hot sex, and mind-numbing alcohol. He didn't expect her to hang around for long after he proved she didn't love Callum unconditionally. And he didn't expect to have an inkling of interest for her tomorrow. The sooner she was gone, the better. There was no way she wanted his brother for keeps. Every woman who'd ever shown interest in him suddenly developed an aversion once they witnessed a full-blown attack of his Tourette's. How could this girl be any different?

"Where do you want to go?"

"Come on." He walked towards the equipment barn. Callum better not have touched his Harley. He'd rebuilt it himself before he left to follow the circuit. When Arden entered the dim interior of the barn, he immediately saw the black tarp in the corner. His heart leapt. There was nothing quite like hitting the open road, feeling the wind rushing by his ears, and the power of the engine beneath him. It had always been his therapy— next to the bottle.

Life wasn't simple. Callum's answer was to isolate himself on the ranch. Arden had tried to spread his wings, but failed. It wasn't easy to stay focused without a goal. He was drifting through life, living for instant gratification. But his capricious lifestyle was catching up with him.

"What is it?" asked Hailey.

"My bike." He whipped off the tarp, frozen in place once he saw the beast.

Her footsteps sounded on the hay-littered concrete as she came closer. "Nice," she said.

"You ever ride one?" He was still spell-bound by the meager light reflecting off the chrome surfaces.

"No way."

The hesitation in her voice piqued his interest. He was squatting down to check that everything appeared functional but stopped and turned to look at her. "You want to take on the wild hogs but you're scared of a little bike?"

He rolled it out of the barn and into the sunlight of the main yard. It was his baby, the only thing of value he owned next to his horse and truck. He threw his leg over the seat and tested the suspension. It felt good, reminding him of old times.

"Does it work?" she asked.

"Of course it works." The key dangled from the ignition where he'd left it. Callum never had Arden's interest of motorcycles, preferring a horse or his pickup truck. He turned the key and revved the engine. It fired to life, a beautiful, healthy sound. "Get on," he said.

"What? I'm not getting on there."

Hailey was too inhibited. She was a good girl,

and he rarely tangled with them. They were too much effort and not nearly as exciting in the bedroom. "Don't be a baby. Just climb on and hang on tight. I'm just going for a quick run."

"I don't know…"

"Come on. It'll be fun. Promise."

She bit her full lower lip, gathering her hair into a makeshift bun. "Is it safe?"

"Trust me."

Hailey cautiously approached. She rested a hand on his bicep while lifting her leg over the seat behind him. Her body was slight but pressed tight to his back.

"Hold on tight." As soon as he hit the gas, her arms snaked around his waist, holding on for her life. It felt good to have a woman's hands on him again. The vibration of the engine travelled through his body, bringing him to life. He couldn't help but smile as he raced down the familiar dirt roads. As a teen he had his dirt bike. It was the same thrill now, one he savored. When he heard Hailey squeal, a jovial sound, he was glad he'd pushed her to come along.

Being on the road was an adventure, always something exciting happening to keep his mind off reality. He was terrified to return home and fall back into the same bleak routine. But now that he witnessed the endless golden fields, and the rich evergreen treeline in the distance, he knew he'd made the right choice to come home.

Hailey's hands gripped his shirt, kneading the muscles in his chest. Arden twisted his wrist, sending the bike speeding along the barren stretch of road. When he finally realized they were only coasting, the roar of the engine extinguished, they were miles from home.

Chapter Eight

"What's wrong?" she asked. Arden steered the bike to the side of the road. The steady drone of crickets filled her ears once the engine quieted.

"I was too damn hasty." He got off the bike and knocked the kick stand down with his boot. "Come on." He helped her off the bike, the sound of gravel crunching under her shoes when she hit the ground.

"Did you run out of gas?"

"Could be. Like I said, I wasn't thinking." His jaw clenched down hard, and he kicked at the weeds growing along the side of the road. *"Fuck."*

She felt awkward, unable to help because she knew nothing about mechanics. After a few minutes Arden returned his attention to the motorcycle, trying to get it running. His waves of dark hair fell over into his eyes, his shirt pulling tight over his shoulders. Hailey couldn't help her physical attraction to the cowboy—or perhaps it was just his similarity to Callum that piqued her interest.

"Do you know if there're any farm houses in the area?"

He exhaled an irritated breath. "Darlin', ain't nothing 'round here but prairie. The closest ranch is back at my place."

"You don't have to yell," she said. "I'm just trying to help."

"Like you're trying to help Callum, by getting *yourself* a grant? Maybe my brother is love-blind, but I'm lucid enough to know nothing in life is free."

"Wow, you're something else." She began to walk away, in the direction of the O'Shea Ranch.

"Fuck. I'm sorry. Stop."

She ignored him, walking a fast clip. There was

nothing wrong with some good, old-fashioned exercise. She just hoped the heat wouldn't kill her.

"Hailey!" She heard his heavy footfalls catching up with her.

"Leave me alone. Why don't you find some comfort in the bottom of your flask?"

His hand wrapped around her upper arm. Arden easily stopped her, spinning her around to face him. "Sometimes I speak before I think. It's a flaw of mine."

"Callum has an excuse for his behavior. You? You have a choice in how you act."

Unlike Callum's dark eyes, Arden's were as blue as the clear sky above them. He forced her to pay attention to him, and she had little choice in her current predicament.

"You're right. I was wrong. But before you judge me, try walking a mile in my shoes. You've seen and heard Callum's symptoms. Imagine them tenfold. He's improved over the years, teaching himself how to mask the tics. Back when we were younger I was fighting nearly every damn day of my life." He tilted up her chin when she tried to look away. "You see, Callum's not a fighter. When he's upset, he internalizes the pain. Me, I lash out."

"That's understandable. You love your brother, so you look out for him. I can respect that."

"Don't you see, darlin'. There ain't nothing wrong with me. But I couldn't in good conscience socialize with people who teased by kid brother. A man has to have some honor."

"You can't use your sacrifice as an excuse forever."

He narrowed his eyes. She knew he was looking for sympathy, but she wouldn't enable his cycle of negative behavior.

"Are all scientists cold-hearted?"

Before she could respond, the sound of an approaching vehicle captured their attention.

A black pickup truck with raised suspension pulled up alongside them. There were three rough and rowdy cowboys inside, a low twang of country music coming from the radio. The driver leaned out the window, a sly smile on his face. "Well, hello there, beautiful. Looks like you may need a ride."

"Our bike broke down," she said. "Could you give us a ride to the O'Shea Ranch?"

"Hailey, don't," whispered Arden. She didn't see what the problem was. If they could get back to the ranch, Arden could get his truck and horse trailer and come back for his motorcycle.

"Listen to your friend, sweetheart. There's only room for one in our truck. I'm sure Arden can manage on his own."

Shit. They knew each other. These were probably some of the bullies Arden and Callum had to deal with.

"Well, if that's the case, I'll walk with Arden."

"What a man. Leads his woman into the boondocks and then forces her to walk. Classy, Arden, as always." The other men laughed inside, the hysterical sound destroying the peaceful serenity of the landscape.

"Maybe you should go," whispered Arden. "If you want to save your feet, it's your best option."

"Listen to the man," said the driver.

She kept walking, shaking her head. "Thanks anyway. But I enjoy walking."

They wouldn't take no for an answer. "Stop playing hard to get. Makes no sense walking when we're offering to drive you."

She was beginning to feel uncomfortable, so she ignored them, looking straight ahead. If Callum were there, he'd stick up for her, make her feel safe.

When they wouldn't drive off, Arden put himself between her and the truck.

"You've heard her, now fuck off." He even stepped up onto the running board with one foot, getting in the face of the driver. "I know where you live, Bradshaw."

The humor fled from the man's face and he hit the gas after Arden stepped down.

He'd surprised her. "Thank you," she said, taking a deep breath once she could only see a billow of dust down the long, narrow dirt road.

Arden stopped her again. "Why'd you do that?"

"Do what?" she asked.

"You could have gotten a ride, but you refused."

"I wasn't about to leave you all alone."

"But I was being an asshole."

"You were just being human. There's nothing wrong with that." She smiled at him, hoping to make amends if possible. Hailey still had to live with Arden and Callum if she was to finish her research. Being on hostile terms would be unpleasant at best.

"You're something different." He stroked her hair, an intimate touch she wasn't expecting. "Pretty, too."

"We should start walking," she said.

"Are you frightened of me?"

Could he feel her body tremble with trepidation and anticipation at once? She desperately wanted the bad boy to want her, to desire her. But she also knew exactly what kind of man he was. He'd use her for all she was worth and discard her faster than she could redress. After finding a potential relationship with Callum O'Shea, she wouldn't jeopardize that for the cowboy drifter. At least Callum showed signs of stability, work ethic, and devotion. She was well aware they were both virtual strangers, but her initial assessment warned her to stay away from Arden.

"A little," she said honestly. Hailey was scared of what he represented, and of her intense attraction to him.

"I've never hurt a woman, and never will. My daddy may have been a volatile man, but he loved our mother something fierce." He slipped his hand around her waist, bringing her a hair's length from his body. "Tell me, lady scientist, does that mean I'm capable of love, too?"

"E–Everyone is capable of love." She could feel the heat of his body and the roughness of his hand against the small band of exposed flesh at her back. Her body reacted, tempting her to give in to his ministrations. But she wouldn't.

"What about you, Ms. Watson. Can you love a sinner?"

Her breath caught. It would be so easy to close her eyes and let him whisk her away to a place only the two of them existed. She imagined he'd be a skilled and attentive lover, even if untamed. Hailey knew the pleasures of the flesh firsthand thanks to Callum, and that knowledge only made Arden more tempting.

"Don't you love your brother?"

He cocked his head. "Of course. Why you asking?"

"You said he's falling in love with me. If that's true, I wonder how he'll feel knowing you're ready to take what he considers his."

He groaned, taking a deep breath before pulling away. Arden massaged behind his neck with both hands while staring at her. "You know what? I was going to fuck you right here, out in the open. That was my whole plan when coming out here. I was going to prove to myself you were no good for my little brother."

"Why?"

"Because he's special! I won't have some money-hungry whore breaking his heart, pretending to love him back while mocking him in her head."

She stopped breathing, her chest tight. He was crude, not holding his tongue for anyone. Was that what Arden thought of her?

"But then you came along and proved me wrong. I didn't think a woman could ever love Callum the way he deserved." He returned to her, trailing his thumb over her lower lip. "You've just complicated my life, baby girl."

They started walking. She hadn't said a word, still trying to decipher everything he'd said. She felt like a leaf being tossed back and forth between the waves and the shore, unable to settle on either. Hailey's heart felt bound to Callum but she had new, intense feelings for his own brother. Maybe she would have been better off living in a cardboard box than showing up at the O'Shea Ranch. They weren't just town outcasts. They managed to work some sort of spell on her, making her incapable of walking away. Visions of Leprechauns danced in her head.

"It's getting hot," he said after they'd walked for what felt like miles. "Too hot."

She nodded, trudging on.

Arden decided to yank off his shirt. He tucked the edge through a loop in his belt and carried on. Unbeknownst to him, his bare upper body was making her ravenous. He had Celtic bands around each developed bicep and a Celtic cross on his right pec. His tattoos only added to his rugged appeal. The more she knew she should stay away, the more she wanted him.

"Want me to carry you?" he asked after a while.

"We're both tired. I'm not going to make you carry me."

"Just for a bit so you can let your feet rest. Besides, there's nothing to you." He stopped, squatting on the ground.

"Arden, no."

"Come on, now."

She mounted his back and he hoisted her up, an arm supporting each thigh. Hailey felt like a child, clinging to his shoulders in fear of falling. He was tall, so the drop wouldn't be pleasant. His skin was warm with a light sheen of sweat. She wanted to splay her fingers and explore his body, but kept her fantasies locked in her mind.

"So, what happens after you get this grant of yours?" he asked, his words labored.

She hadn't really thought about it. Hailey had been so busy trying to survive day to day, running from the past, that the future rarely plagued her thoughts. A grant only meant she could pay her rent and put food on the table. It didn't equate a home, love, or a job that challenged her. Breaking into the human behavioral branch without a decade of experience was nearly impossible. Studying horses and hogs was as good as she could get in the meantime, but the pay was lackluster.

"I need grants because getting a job as a professor or funding for anything meaningful won't happen for a long, long time."

"Me and Callum only finished high school. We would have dropped out but our mother insisted on having our diplomas hanging on the wall. With my brother's Tourette's and the heavy work load of the farm, it's a miracle we made it through, but we did."

"What about you? Are you staying home for good

or leaving again?" she asked.

"I don't know. I rarely think beyond tomorrow."

After another fifteen minutes of being carried along the side of the road, Arden began to stagger. He ended up bending over and spilling her onto the soft, grassy meadow. He dropped to his back, laying a forearm across his eyes. They were both laughing out loud, both exhausted and overheated. Their predicament was so horrible, the only thing left was to find humor in it.

"Sorry, baby girl. I can't carry you another minute. That mid-day sun is brutal."

"I know. My clothes are soaked through."

"It feels good doing nothing and not feeling anxious about it. I think you're my new good luck charm."

"Your new drug of choice?" she teased. Even with the heat he didn't reach for the flask he'd kept in his back pocket.

As they rested there on the grass, studying the odd white cloud that drifted by, she felt a soul-deep connection with Arden. There was a quiet acceptance between them. Any man could put on a good show but they were all human beneath the tough exterior. She was curious about Arden and eager to meet his approval.

The rumble of a vehicle stole their attention. Arden leaned up on his elbows while Hailey sat up straight. She hoped it wasn't the same truckload of jerks. As the pickup truck neared, it slowed down, finally pulling to the side of the road.

"Well, look who's going to save the day," he said.

It was Callum. He came around the front of his truck and shook his head as he neared. "You okay, Hailey?"

"I'm fine. Just tired from walking."

"Didn't you keep gas in my Harley?" asked Arden.

"What on Earth for? It's not mine, and I never expected you back."

"Well, it's broken down a few miles back."

Callum bent over and scooped her up off the ground like she weighed ten pounds. He cradled her in his capable arms and kissed her forehead. "Next time, don't bother with Arden. You're lucky you didn't pass out from the heat."

He carried her back to the truck, but she couldn't help but peer over his shoulder for Arden. He'd hoisted himself off the ground, following behind at a slower clip.

The last door slammed shut and the three of them drove back to the ranch. It was eerily quiet at first, until Arden spoke up. "You can't stay mad at me forever, Callum. I never should have run off like I did, but I wasn't thinking straight at the time."

"You're supposed to be older and wiser, but I was the one left with all the responsibilities."

"Well, I'm back. We're family and that means everything to me. I'll make it up to you," he assured.

She noted Callum's tenseness easing somewhat. Hailey hoped they'd make amends. It wasn't right for two brothers to be at each other's throats when she knew they loved each other. It only cemented the fact that she could never come between them.

Chapter Nine

When they arrived back at the ranch, Callum helped Hailey out of the truck and into his arms. She looked exhausted, her face flush and hairline moist. The poor thing needed to cool off in a hurry. He couldn't believe Arden would be so careless, taking a woman out into nowhere on a bike he hadn't ridden in a year. It was foolhardy—especially when Callum considered Hailey his responsibility.

"Where you taking me?" she asked. He loved holding her close, caring for her. It was something new to him as he'd only ever had to worry about himself. Now he enjoyed the new responsibility. She gave him purpose and hope.

"To cool off."

She was about to question him again but closed her mouth and leaned her head against his chest. Before he'd headed out in search of Hailey, not finding her in the house, he'd cleaned and refilled the main water trough behind the barn. Without air-conditioning in the house, he planned to dunk her in the cool water and then bring her inside for some fresh lemonade.

Arden joined them, leaning against the side of the barn, one boot bent up against the wooden slats. It appeared he knew Callum's plan, but they always did seem to read each other's thoughts growing up. Arden could sense when he wasn't at ease, signaling that a Tourette's attack was imminent. He'd always looked out for Callum, so it would be foolish to stay mad at his big brother. He loved him more than anything—he was blood, family, his best friend.

"Don't think about it, just do it. She's burning up. Same as me," said Arden.

It was one of the hottest days of the year. He

lowered Hailey into the oversized metal tub, clothes and all. As soon as she broke the surface, she latched onto his neck and let out a squeal.

"Callum!"

"Hush now. It's for your own good. I won't have you sick with heat." He continued to settle her into the water until everything but her head was submerged.

"It's freezing!"

Arden set one knee on the grass and lowered his hand into the water. He wet his face and bare chest, well aware what the heat could do to a man. After working on the prairies all their lives, they'd lived through just about every medical and environmental emergency.

When Hailey tried to climb out, struggling to right herself, Arden placed a palm against her stomach. "Settle, little lady. Callum's taking good care of you. Better than I ever could."

The way his brother spoke carried a hint of sadness. Callum had originally been angry that Arden had abandoned him and then for taking Hailey out on an unsafe bike, but he still didn't want him upset. It was time to leave the past in the past and look to the future. Now that Hailey had walked into Callum's life, he actually saw a future for himself. She was a Godsend, a beautiful woman who didn't judge him for his differences. She was like a breath of fresh air.

"Better?" he asked.

"I'm so cold," she said, raising her arms out of the water, reaching for him. He hoisted her out, her body twice as heavy as water rushed down from her soaked clothing.

"Let's get you dried off and hydrated. No more foolish stunts either. One of these days you'll get yourself killed."

"Don't bring her in wet," said Arden as they

approached the side door of the house. Hailey looked over at his brother who walked alongside him. He sensed a connection between her and Arden he never knew existed. But she was unlike any of the women they'd ever tangled with.

He set Hailey down, wondering if she'd cast her spell on Arden as well. His brother had always been a playboy, never keeping a girl for more than a couple weeks. Now he'd come home, maybe to start a new page in life. It would be a blessing if they could work together like they used to, preserving the family ranch. Only things would be different now…because of Hailey. There would be no love loss and loneliness.

How would things be different for Arden though? He'd likely leave if he had to endure the same unfulfilling lifestyle. What if Hailey had eyes for Arden, too? Could Callum actually share his woman with his kin? The concept of sharing went against every fiber of his being. Cowboys were possessive to a fault and Callum was the worst of them. But Arden was his other half, the only man he trusted and loved since his father. The more he digested the idea, the more he realized it wouldn't feel wrong to share with Arden. In fact, the idea began to intrigue him, seemingly too perfect. Hailey could be the binding agent to bring his small family together again.

****

"Take off your clothes," said Arden.

She immediately looked to Callum, expecting him to defend her, to warn his brother to back off. Instead, he nodded once, urging her to comply.

The prospect of stripping in front of two men was titillating. Her body was still wanton from her time with Arden. And she was getting cold and clammy in her sopping wet clothes. Hailey lifted the shirt over her head, letting it drop heavily to the ground. The balmy air tickled her exposed flesh. Only her bra hid her breasts from full view. The strength of the sun helped warm her damp skin, encouraging her to slip out of her pants as well.

"She has a beautiful body," said Arden, his eyes roving over her exposed flesh.

"Trust me, I know it. I just have to think of her to get uncomfortable in the tractor. It makes for long days in the fields knowing she's waiting for me."

"I wager she's worth the wait," said Arden. "Maybe thirty-two years' worth."

Why were they agreeing? She'd pegged Callum as the type to have a jealous streak. In fact, both men were hardcore, Irish cowboys with dominant personalities.

She didn't question them or complain. Hailey felt a budding love for Callum and her attraction for Arden was undeniable. What if they both wanted her? Such a relationship seemed impossible in their day and age, but the men were already ousted from society, making rules of their own.

They both approached, each tall and broad, eyes focused with deadly intent.

"What?" she asked, looking back and forth at the men. Arden's hair was wet from the water, his upper body still gloriously bare. Callum lifted his Stetson off his head and licked his thick lips. He looked hungry, like he had when they first made love.

"I love her, Arden," he said while still looking at her. Her heart skipped a beat hearing the words from his own mouth.

"I know. She's different."

"No playing games," Callum said in warning.

They spoke as if she wasn't there, as if they were

planning a shopping list, not double-teaming her body. She must be misinterpreting.

"I taught you everything you know, little brother." Arden slipped the strap of her bra off her shoulder.

"Not everything," said Callum. He cupped her breast as the material of her bra slid off to expose her nudity. Her nipples had already pebbled from the mix of chill and lust.

The decision appeared to be made, an unspoken confirmation passing between the two men. They were like a team, moving and acting as if they'd rehearsed every touch. The more they dared to advance, the more forceful they became. They reminded her of sharks getting a taste of blood. She welcomed their animalistic behavior. Arden slid her panties down, leaving her completely naked and vulnerable.

Part of her was thrilled that Callum allowed Arden to participate, bringing her fantasy to realization. But did it mean his commitment to her was weak? Was she a sexual object rather than relationship material in his eyes? She pushed her worries aside and savored the feel of their hands worshiping her body. They felt warm and strong, knowing where to touch and not to touch. So far her pussy had been avoided, allowing her time to liquefy, molten heat slipping down her inner thigh.

"Callum…" She ran her hand through his short, dark hair as he trailed kissed down the center of her breast bone. Only last week she'd been a virgin. Now her entire world had opened up, exposing her to the wickedest erotic experiences.

"I thought the townsfolk would have warned you about coming here. We're to be avoided at all costs, or didn't you hear?" asked Arden, tugging her head back by a handful of her hair. He stared into her eyes as his brother travelled lower down her body, his lips grazing her sensitive flesh.

"I'm not afraid. I want you both." Her words felt foreign after she'd spoken. She hoped she hadn't offended Callum or said the wrong thing aloud. Maybe this was another test and she'd failed by desiring both brothers. She couldn't help her human nature, or ignore the little voice inside her head that screamed both men were meant to be hers.

"I've never shared a woman," said Callum.

"It'll be a first for all of us." Arden descended on her lips, crushing his mouth to hers. He tasted masculine, addicting. She kissed him back, not even concerned with breathing at this point. His stubble scraped her cheeks and his fingers combed through her hair, holding her head in place.

How had this happened? Hailey felt as if she were having an out of body experience—floating, soaring, being carried along on the waves of lust. The O'Shea men may be cowboy outcasts, but she wanted nothing more. She just hoped their ménage would stand the test of time. At this point she wasn't sure it would last the night.

"Are you still cold?" asked Arden.

"I'm hot." She felt like an inferno was building in her cunt, growing and spreading out to her extremities. Hailey ran her hands over Arden's shoulders and chest, savoring the firmness of his muscles. He was larger than life, visibly perfect and beyond tempting. Wicked thoughts flitted in her head. She wanted the cowboy duo to take control of her body, make her theirs. Any inhibitions she may have had fled the moment they both agreed to share.

Callum's tongue swiped up her folds, startling her. The intensity was all consuming, making her knees weak. She couldn't believe he'd just licked her pussy. And she wanted more. He secured her hips with his big hands, suckling her clit and exploring with his lively tongue. The sensations were electric. Each time Callum would clear his throat, the brief respite only added to her growing bliss.

Arden grabbed her wrist and brought it to the front of his black jeans. His cock was ramrod hard, making her gasp. He smirked, a devilish tilt of the lips. "You have no idea what you're in store for, sweetheart."

She was tempted to tell him not to hurt her. Two men invading her body was a daunting prospect. But she bit her tongue, knowing she'd welcome that kind of pain right now—craved it even.

Callum stood up, towering over her. Her pussy felt empty and achy, in desperate need of attention. Side by side, her dark-haired cowboys made her heart race and inner walls tighten. They studied her curves, their eyes glazed over in lust. She hoped they liked what they saw. Hailey had always been a conservative girl, only concerned with her studies. Now she was standing in the yard of the ranch, without a stitch of clothing, acres of open prairie in all directions. She never wanted to return to her old self or old life.

Callum removed his shirt and then slid his leather belt out of his Wranglers. The sound of the buckle made her nipples tighten. She wondered what it would feel like to be punished by him, to be turned over his knee and spanked like a naughty child.

"We best get her inside before things get carried away." Callum scooped her up into his arms. His chest was warm against her skin, and his strength continually aroused her.

"So, I take it you're not mad at your brother anymore?"

He kissed her temple. "I can't stay mad at him. He's all I have left." She wanted to say that he had her, but she kept quiet.

Callum didn't bring her upstairs as she expected. Instead, he sat down on the larger sofa and cradled her on his lap.

"Touch me, darlin'. I wanna feel your little hand on my cock," said Callum.

Hailey loved when his rawness made its appearance. Day to day, he was a sweetheart with old-fashioned values. Once the heat turned up he transformed into a man possessed. She shifted to her knees and straddled his legs. The cooler air caressed her slick folds once her thighs were parted wide. Hailey was excited, anxious, and had never been so horny. She unbuttoned his pants with both hands and then lowered his zipper. When she slid her hand inside, searching for the virile length of flesh, Arden squeezed her ass from behind. Her breath caught.

"Don't worry about him," said Callum. "Keep on going."

Hailey tried her best to ignore Arden's probing hands and continued to release Callum's erection. She'd never had a chance to see it up close. It was darker than the rest of his body with thick, bulging veins. It was an instrument made for her pleasure and she explored it with fondness, her curiosity aroused.

"You're so big," she said. "I can't believe that was inside of me."

"Now imagine two," Arden whispered from behind. He licked the shell of her ear, sending shivers skittering along her skin. "Does that excite you?"

She nodded, dropping her head back.

"Stroke it, Hailey. Don't stop touching me."

She was pulled in two directions, needing and

wanting both men at the same time. Doing as asked, she gripped Callum and began to pump her fist. It amazed her how his cock thickened before her eyes, becoming even more intimidating.

"Good girl," said Arden. "Now climb up and sit on him."

She swallowed hard, the mix of anticipation and apprehension only making her pussy clamp down more. Hailey braced her hands on Callum's shoulders and rose up high enough so he could aim himself directly at her entrance. Her breathing picked up as he slid the head of his cock back and forth to moisten himself. Every touch only teased her at this point.

"Okay, take it all, darlin'." He held the base of his erection as she ever so slowly impaled herself on his monster cock. She should have known he'd be well endowed by the size of his cowboy boots. He filled every inch of her, leaving no cell untouched. She tightened around him, reveling in the fullness.

She leaned forward now, yearning for intimacy, not just sex. Being connected with Callum was special to her, not just a joining of the bodies. She kissed his neck, unable to control her need to devour him.

"Sweet, baby girl. You're all ours," Callum murmured, his arms wrapped around the small of her back. She could feel his cock pulsing inside her, raring to go. "I'm never letting you go."

Ours. The single word was confirmation of her two most fundamental questions—they'd claimed her and they planned to share her.

She was startled when Callum's palm came down on one side of her ass. The solid sound echoed in the room.

"You're on top, Hailey. You have to work his cock on your own," said Arden, his hand smoothing up and down her back. He had one knee on the sofa beside Callum, his clothes completely off. She turned her head enough to see him stroking his own cock. He was huge. That mysterious trail of dark hair she'd admired all morning and afternoon led to something she never expected.

She was still so inexperienced but eager to learn everything. Hailey began to lift her weight up and down over Callum's cock. Every minor stroke increased the heat building inside her. Her eyes lolled back in her head from the pressure and pending orgasm.

Callum assisted her once she worked up a consistent rhythm. He gripped her hips, helping her rise and fall over his hardened flesh. Each time she'd drop down, she'd let out a groan. The delicious friction made her nearly delirious. She wanted to drop her weight and allow him to lead her.

"It feels...so good," she managed to say. Arden watched her, monitoring her expressions and reactions. She felt dirty and uninhibited, the dark side of her desires unleashed. "I want more."

She knew her request would be met. It was a carefully decided moment because she was aware there'd be no turning back. She'd have to woman up and take two extremely ready males.

She felt a cool, lubricated finger press against her asshole. It stunned her for a moment before she realized it was Arden preparing her rear entrance. The forbidden touch was surprisingly erotic, thousands of tiny pinprick sensations firing to life.

"Don't tighten, Hailey. Just relax. Focus on Callum's dick, not my finger." Even in their heightened arousal, they still took the time to fully prepare her. The gesture put her at ease and made her affection for the men grow.

It was hard to ignore the probing finger which quickly turned into two. He scissored his moist fingers, stretching her stubborn sphincter muscle. After studying science for years, she knew human anatomy well. She was aware, medically, that her virgin ass could take Arden's full length with no ill effects if he was well lubricated. She had to relax and not tense up. Arden may not have gone to college but he certainly knew the rules when it came to sex. She suspected by the end of the night, he'd be able to teach her a thing or two.

Chapter Ten

Sex had never meant much to Arden. It was a means of sexual release and short-term entertainment. But for the first time he was fully engaged, anticipating every moment with the passion of his youth. He'd never found a woman who gave him pause—until now. Hailey was sweet, down to Earth, and didn't judge like a typical woman. Callum had chosen well.

At first he'd been happy for his brother. His life had been a constant challenge and he deserved to find love and peace. Now Arden saw the potential of the same peace for himself. Could the little blonde scientist be the woman to tame him? What would life on the family ranch be with a woman under foot? Could the years finally be worth living for Arden and his younger brother? He suspected Hailey could be the answer, but he was still wary.

Her mewling sounds fueled him, filling his head, his lungs, and his heart with her essence. He began to kiss her back, preparing to engage her body. Never in his life had he shared a woman with his brother or any other man. The idea was erotic but unnatural. However, from the second the decision had been made, it was like their threesome was meant to be, the answer to the major setbacks in their lives. He was as comfortable with Callum as he was in his own skin. Sharing a woman was the most logical progression if they wanted a future together on the O'Shea Ranch—one worth living.

Although part of him was like a rider at the starting gates, full of hope and pumped up on adrenaline, another part was terrified to lower his guards. He'd been rejected all his life. First, for being Callum's brother, the boy everyone considered either demon-possessed or retarded. Then for the person the townsfolk turned him into—an outcast who lived for fighting. Violence was in his blood, and he fought well. If it wasn't to defend his brother, it was to punish assholes that pissed him off. The more the town hated him, the more he retreated from regular society.

Having Hailey enter their darkly masculine world, rarely treaded on by outsiders, was a unique gift. She was unique, intelligent, and appeared to care about their plight.

"Get ready for me," he said. Hailey was the picture of innocence, which only aroused him more. The women he tangled with left much to be desired. Hailey was everything he never expected to attain in a partner.

"Yes," she said, her breathing heavy. She was close, her cries becoming louder the longer Callum worked her over his cock.

Arden made sure he was thoroughly lubricated before pushing the head of his cock against her tight asshole. The fact she was willing to accept both of them, two men nobody else wanted, made his heart swell.

"You're fucking tight, baby girl." He definitely didn't want to hurt her. She trusted them and he wouldn't break that confidence. And if he ever wanted to double-team her with Callum again, she needed to remember this day fondly. "Tell me how you feel."

"Oh God... I feel so full."

"That's because there're two cocks inside you." He'd only entered her an inch, the worst of the experience. Once she stretched wide enough, there would be no discomfort. "Relax and take it all."

He braced one knee on the sofa as he attempted to force more of his cock into her tight ass. Callum's erection was a roadblock he had to slide against to fill her, only a thin membrane separating them. The resulting snugness nearly made him come on the spot.

"I love you, darlin'," said Callum. His brother had committed body and soul. He prayed this little angel wasn't a devil in disguise. Good things were a rarity in their lives.

Once he was fully seated, he exhaled. He was using immeasurable control to go slow for her first ménage. There was no way she'd had a man before Callum.

"Hurry up, Arden. I can't hold off much longer," said Callum, working with him to piston in and out of her body like a finely tuned machine.

They fucked her hard, thrusting in her pussy and ass. She contracted around Arden's cock in spontaneous bursts. It wouldn't be much longer for her. He toyed with her tits from behind, rolling her nipple against the pad of his finger.

"I–I can't take it anymore," she said.

"Then let it all go. Come for us," said Arden.

She could scarcely speak, her breathing heavier than an athlete's. "I can't…"

"Come!" he demanded, his cock swelling inside her. He was about to release when she detonated. Her ass clamped down hard, waves of contractions following. He spilled inside her, his orgasm nearly blinding, lingering on and on and on.

She screamed, the desperate sound testament to a positive experience. He kissed her shoulder blade as he carefully slipped out of her ass.

He felt uniquely vulnerable, his emotions all over the place. Arden decided to leave the two lovebirds alone while he made a quick exit.

****

"Hunting hogs again?" asked Arden. He led his horse behind him, his spurs chiming with each step. The underbrush parted as he approached.

"Shhh," she said. "I'm testing something new. It uses sound waves." Well over a month had gone by since their ménage was solidified. Their lives meshed into one effortlessly.

Hailey had been staking out the edge of the forest all morning. She knew the hog trails and feeding grounds. It was only a matter of time until one of her theories panned out.

He sauntered around the area, finally leaning against a tree. Arden chewed on a piece of wheat, watching her. He only wore a pair of worn Wranglers and an unbuttoned plaid shirt. The strength of the sun didn't reach them under the forest canopy. It was cooler here than out in the fields, a private place she learned to appreciate. The solitude and sounds of nature were soothing.

"Interesting." He smirked. Hailey knew he wasn't interested in the intricacies of her research. But he'd taken time out of his daily duties to stop by and see her. Coming from Arden, it meant a lot.

"Sure, Arden." She smiled back, her body sizzling just from his proximity. He looked at her with those narrowed blue eyes, nearly bringing her to her knees.

"I'm here to help, baby girl. Use me any way you see fit."

She had many inappropriate ideas, but pushed them away. Tonight she'd have both her cowboys at her disposal. "Can you hang this up in that branch?" She passed him one of the recorders she used to emit the signals.

As he reached up, there was a rustling in the branches to their left. It was a wild boar. She immediately jumped behind Arden, her fear of the beasts just as strong as when one nearly attacked her.

"Relax. I won't let it hurt you. You want me to kill it?"

"No," she snapped. "Just…just scare it away."

Arden ran through the underbrush towards the hog, yelling and stomping his feet. The animal took off, scampering away faster than it appeared. Arden looked comical, making light of her fears.

"That work for you, sugar?" He had a healthy glow, the smile transforming his face. In the last couple months he'd transformed from an aloof drunk to a committed rancher. He made small gestures each day, the same as Callum. They made her feel like a princess.

"I guess." She stepped closer, unable to keep her distance. *Just one touch.*

"I think you've had enough research for one day. Come home with me."

"Later. I'm so close."

He shook his head. "Wrong answer." He bent over and tossed her over his shoulder, smacking her ass. "You have to learn balance. Time for work and time for play."

"And I'm guessing you want to play?"

"I just saved your life, darlin'. I should get a little something, no?"

"Fine, I'll suck your cock. Then you have to let me be for a couple hours."

He set her down on her feet. "Deal." He kissed her, a kiss so passionate, her folds instantly moistened.

In the shadows of leafy lacework, she dropped to her knees and unzipped his Wranglers. She loved being his one and only, the woman he came to when he had urges. His cock was beautiful, her own personal play thing—and she had two. Hailey wrapped her lips around him, savoring his guttural sounds. He held her hair, guiding her over his thick erection.

"Good girl," he said. "I'll pay you back tonight. I can't wait to suck your sweet, little pussy." His words spurred her on. She took him deeper, faster, gagging slightly from his size. He smelled like his musky cologne and horses. The cool, damp earth penetrated the knees of her jeans, but she didn't falter until he released in her mouth. He loved it when she swallowed him so she obliged him, licking her lips when she was through.

****

"I've got it!" Hailey shouted, as she ran out to Callum's pickup truck. He was just about to head into town to pick up supplies at the general store—sugar, coffee, salt, and he wanted to get something pretty for Hailey.

She climbed up the running board and leaned into the open window.

"What's going on?"

"I've done it. I've solved the hog problem." She spoke so fast, he had difficulty understanding her. "It may have taken me longer than expected, but I did it."

She was as giddy as a schoolgirl, her smile contagious. What he initially expected to take a couple of weeks, took two months. He never questioned her extended stay because he never wanted her to leave. She was his, the reason for him to get up in the morning. The thought of losing that joy was indigestible.

"Tell me."

"I mixed two synthetic scent markers—bear and wolf. I marked the treeline of the field they love to dig up. And it worked!" She leaned in further and kissed him on the lips. "I'm just writing up my research report and proposal now."

"Proposal?"

"For my grant. They have to fund my research now. Do you realize what this means?"

It meant the dozens of farmers in the area, and hundreds in the neighboring communities, would have a safe, effective solution to the hog problem. It would keep them out of specific areas so farmers could be profitable once again. It also meant he could lose the best thing in his life. He was flooded with mixed feelings.

Callum was happy for Hailey. She'd accomplished what she'd set out to do, and he was proud. But their relationship had grown and strengthened over the past couple months. He'd never seen his brother happier, and there was no more talk about leaving or following the circuit from Arden. It seemed they'd all found paradise in their own bubble of time and space away from the rest of the world. Would he lose it all now?

"You did good, sweetheart." He squeezed the steering wheel repeatedly, trying to stave off a full blown attack of his Tourette's. Hailey was his rock, never judging, always understanding, even in the worst of circumstances. She made him feel normal, made him feel like a man. He couldn't lose her.

"You heading into town?"

"I have a few supplies to get and I have to pick up Arden from the distribution center. He sold his bike, so he needs a ride home."

"Sold his bike? But he loved that motorcycle."

"People change. It was his decision."

Three, two, one. One, two, three. Three, two, one.

She climbed into the passenger seat and they headed off to town. He wondered how long it would take her to write up her research papers. He hoped it took another two months but doubted it.

The roads were dusty. So far the summer had been brutal, borderline drought conditions. "I'm mighty proud, Hailey. You worked hard to get those results. I never would have thought of half the things you tried."

"I just had to get into their heads, think like a boar. They're territorial animals, and once they smelled the scent of a natural predator it warned them to stay away."

"Just brilliant, darlin'." For once he sympathized with the hogs. His territorial nature was flaring within him, terrified to lose the woman he considered his.

They first stopped off and picked up Arden. He slid into the passenger side, sandwiching her between them.

"Why'd you do it, Arden? Why'd you sell your bike?"

He kissed her forehead, not answering her question.

"You loved that bike," she said, not letting the topic drop.

"It was just a thing. Things can be replaced. People can't." Arden cupped her cheek, kissing her lips. "I have something to think about besides myself now." She stopped challenging him and gave in to his ministrations.

Their threesome was so natural. He never had an inkling of jealousy for his brother. Any other cowboy was another story entirely, and they both watched over her like hawks when they visited town. She belonged on the O'Shea Ranch and he never wanted that status to change.

The general store was busier than usual. He guessed the customers were stocking up for the upcoming long weekend. Normally he'd drive away and come back when things were quieter, but that wasn't easy to explain to Hailey. He didn't want her to see him as different.

She hooked arms with Arden as they entered the

store. Callum came up the rear, cautious of his surroundings and fully aware that he had a new, aggressive vocal tic. It was loud, atypical, and difficult to control. He counted down from one hundred as he entered the store, anything to keep his mind occupied and off his Tourette's. At least he had Arden and Hailey with him—his two rocks.

He found the sugar on a back shelf and then the salt. Arden and Hailey found the rest.

"Can we get some shampoo and conditioner?" she asked Arden when they approached the counter to pay. She'd run out of her girly supplies weeks earlier and had to use their masculine alternatives.

"You get whatever you like, baby doll," said Arden, all over her like white on rice. Neither of them could get enough of their little scientist. She wore a simple cotton dress today, accentuating her youthful beauty. Her dirty-blonde hair hung loose down her back, tucked behind her ears.

There were people everywhere—beside him, behind him, scattered throughout the store. The cashier stared at him as if he was the son of Satan himself.

"I need the strawberry shampoo...sh–ampoo...sh–ampoo..." *Fuck, fuck, fuck.* He couldn't even function like a normal human being. He wanted to crawl into a hole and never emerge. The worst of it was Hailey watching him make a fool of himself, and he knew it was only the beginning. Now that he'd started a new tic, it wouldn't let up, especially when he felt so stressed and under the microscope.

"One strawberry shampoo and one conditioner, please," said Hailey, her fingers closing around his hand. His throat clogged with emotion. How much could he love a woman?

He could hear the whispers all around. Callum

was used to it but wished he could be invisible to their gossip.

After they'd paid, a man dressed in a casual suit stopped Hailey. He must have seen the whole display. "Long time no see," he said. "I heard you were busy with your research."

"Yes, sir. I'll actually be sending in a new proposal soon. I think you'll be pleasantly surprised this time, Mr. Fischer."

"I look forward to it." The older man eyed Callum and Arden skeptically and then went on his way. He'd managed to keep quiet while Hailey spoke with the man. He only wished he could fit into her world, be accepted by the people she respected. It would never be reality for him.

They exited the store, starting the short walk to the truck.

"Run while you can, darlin'. Get yourself a real man." The voice originated from a group of three cowboys standing out front of the general store as they exited. Hailey ignored them. Callum ignored them. Arden didn't.

****

Hailey had wanted to hold onto Callum and never let go when they were in the store. He always struggled in public places and she wished she could shelter him from the world. It was the look of humiliation in his dark eyes that broke her heart. It wasn't his fault. It was society that needed to be educated and more tolerant of others.

It seemed every other time they came into town there was a confrontation of some sort. Callum usually withdrew into himself, more embarrassed than angry. Today they had Arden with them. The usually cool and controlled Irish cowboy lost it.

He yanked off his plaid long-sleeved shirt, which he wore unbuttoned over his black tank top. He tossed it to the dusty sidewalk and stormed over to the group of men, not a hint of apprehension in his step.

"What did you say to our woman?"

"*Our* woman? You two wouldn't know conventional if it dropped out of the sky and hit you on the head, would you?" the tallest man said.

"You all need to fuck off and mind your own business. Last I heard this was still a free country."

"Arden…" she warned. Hailey didn't want him to do anything he'd regret. The three cowboys leaning against the glass windows of the store looked unsavory.

The tall man laughed, the other two following suit. "She even has to stick up for them. How pathetic can two men get? When are ya'll going to realize you're not wanted in these parts? We're God-fearing citizens in this town."

Arden's muscled flexed, his Celtic bands moving as his biceps shifted. She didn't want him to get into trouble because of a few ignorant jerks.

"You've never walked a mile in my shoes. God-fearing has nothing to do with it because He abandoned us long ago. So I have no reservations about fucking all three of you up."

"Just like your father," said the man with the tan cowboy hat. He spat on the ground beside him. According to Arden and Callum, their parents were always outcast as the unwanted Irish immigrants. It seemed that hatred carried through the generations in the backwards little town.

Arden charged forward, driving his fist into the gut of the cowboy. His body was lean and powerful, and as much as she was worried, she knew he'd come out on top.

"Callum, do something!" she cried.

He only shook his head. "He likes it, darlin'. Just leave him be." Callum wrapped his arm around her, keeping her safe and close. If things got out of hand, she knew Callum would step in. But if she knew Arden, and she did, he needed to let off the steam he'd been building up.

A gunshot fired off, bringing the area to deafening silence. The small crowd that had gathered froze, and the vicious fight ceased. A lone cowboy with a pot belly stepped forward, holding his rifle in warning.

"Why don't you two get back to your God-forsaken ranch and stay out of town. You're both nothing but trouble."

Arden picked up his shirt and black Stetson, swatting it across his jeans to clear the dust from the scuffle. "And a lovely day to you too, Mr. Anderson," said Arden. As the three of them returned to the truck, he turned around. "And you ain't the only one who knows how to use a rifle." He winked mockingly.

"Don't aggravate him," Callum said. "We've got what we need. No more trouble."

When they were out of sight and back at the truck, Arden slammed the heel of his hand against the side. "I can't believe those assholes. They can't leave well enough alone."

"You only encourage them by reacting," she said.

"How can I help it? They disrespected my brother and my woman. I won't fucking have it!"

His woman. The two words sounded like a dream. As much as the townspeople may reject Callum and Arden O'Shea, she felt like the luckiest woman in the world. Her men were drop-dead gorgeous, excellent lovers, attentive, loving, and fun to be with. She'd always been a loner herself, focused on her research, so living off the grid wouldn't be a drastic change for her. If living on the fringe of society was a prerequisite for her ménage relationship, she'd gladly accept it. It was a small consolation to finding love in the arms of her two cowboy heroes.

Chapter Eleven

Hailey had all her papers together. She stuffed them into her knapsack and then pulled out of the driveway in her noisy old truck. With both men working together in the fields, she didn't want to disturb them. After finally achieving her goal and pounding out the most convincing essay she could, the idea of waiting even another day to turn in her proposal wasn't an option.

As she drove the back roads to the university, she realized she was more excited to make Arden and Callum proud. Her focus no longer lingered on her proving her parents wrong or trying to show up her professors. Her entire life had shifted course, giving her a new drive and purpose.

After turning her papers into Professor Fischer, he asked her to wait outside his office while he consulted with two other faculty members. She'd paced the halls for three quarters of an hour before the door opened. Her heart skipped a beat when she saw the professor wave her to enter.

"Have a seat, Ms. Watson."

She felt awkward and on display, the three men staring at her like a slide on a microscope.

"We're very impressed with your new proposal. It seems you had something worth taking notice in after all."

She swallowed hard and kept quiet.

"After careful consideration, we've decided to offer you a very lucrative position in Jacksburg County. You'll head up a new division in their university."

Her mouth dropped open. This was everything a young scientist could dream of. It felt impossible, like she'd wake up from a dream. Then the reality slowly trickled into her mind. Jacksburg was half way across the country in a thriving city, nothing like her current little town. How could she leave Arden and Callum? There was no way they'd leave their ranch and she'd never ask it of them. Her initial excitement plummeted.

"Thank you very much. I don't know what to say."

"It would be wise to say yes. We'll need your answer by the end of tomorrow," said Professor Fischer.

She left the office and wandered the halls aimlessly, finally heading for the second level where she still had a locker on loan. Hailey wanted to pick up her remaining books and notes she'd left behind. It must have been between classes because the hallways were suddenly swarming with students heading in one direction or the other. She felt like a lifeless body carried along on the sea.

When she reached her locker, she froze. There was graffiti across the front of her locker, the others untouched. In red letters it read, *Mick Freak Lover.*

Hailey wasn't sure how long she stood there like a rock in a river, the students passing around her, whispering and giggling.

"I'll get the janitor to come clean it."

She turned around to find her good friend, Peter. It had only been a couple months since she'd seen him, but he looked older, more mature. His career had just started to take off when she moved in with the O'Shea men.

"What's it mean?" she asked, staring at the words.

"Nothing. It's a derogatory word for Irishman, but don't think anything of it. It's just some students being stupid."

"We were those students a couple years ago,

Pete."

They weren't dealing with high school students. These were adults, and apparently news in a small town spread like wildfire.

"Come here. I need to talk to you." He dragged her through the throngs of students to an empty classroom, closing the door behind them.

She was afraid to hear what he had to say, didn't want to acknowledge any of the drawbacks to her decision to live with the O'Shea men.

"What are you doing, Hales?" He held both her arms to stop her from pacing.

"What?"

"You've gone off the deep end. The entire community is blathering on about the promising young scientist throwing her career away to hook up with the cowboy outcasts."

"Cowboy outcasts? Really?" Did Peter actually fall for the gossip?

"Don't tell me you've never heard of them. You've always been one to investigate everything, to reach conclusions with logic rather than emotion. What happened to you?"

She fell in love. She found purpose. Hailey shrugged.

"Don't throw away your career. I know Fischer offered you a major opportunity. Don't blow it."

"But—"

"Since you didn't care to look into their history, you should be aware that they go through women faster than you used to devour research texts. You're the flavor of the month, Hales. I don't want to see you hurt."

"I know what I'm doing," she said, tugging herself free from his grasp. At least she hoped to God she knew what she was doing. She still had a huge decision to make, and wasn't sure what to do. What if Peter was right? The O'Shea men had a bad reputation for a reason. What if they tired of her and she lost her one chance at a rewarding career? But what if it was love? Could she actually say good-bye to the two men that controlled her heart? It came down to a primary question—what was more important in life? Money and success or love?

****

"Where is she?" asked Callum. Her piece of shit truck was missing, but she hadn't said anything about needing to head into town. A deep sense of unease whirled around inside him. He'd expected this day but still hoped it would never come.

"You heard her yesterday. Her research is over. She was writing up her proposal all night. I suspect our usefulness is up." Arden tossed his coil of rope over the fence post and disappeared into the barn. Callum followed.

"That doesn't bother you?"

Arden shrugged. "What did I always tell you, Callum? Never fall in love. The last good woman died with our mother."

"You know that's not true. You can play nonchalant all you want, but I know you love her the same as me."

Arden grabbed the shovel they used for mucking out and began to work like a man possessed, putting all his energy into his task. He knew Arden was hurting, but he continually bottled things up rather than admit the truth.

"I'm a free agent," said Arden.

"And I suppose you're going back on the road now, risking your life in the ring. Maybe hit the bottle? You're more fickle than a bitch in heat."

His brother tossed the handle of the shovel and it

clattered to the concrete floor of the barn. He faced off with Callum, chest to chest. "Watch your tone, little brother."

"You blame me for the town judging us, but who's the one feeding into the stereotype? You've been a drunk and a brawler since high school."

"Fuck you!"

Arden was about to throw a punch, but whirled away instead. They were both lost, nothing, not without the woman who made them feel special, wanted, needed.

Callum hoped Hailey was out running errands, but Arden's presumption weighed heavily on his heart. Had she finally had enough of them and their reclusive lifestyle? She'd achieved her goal. What woman would choose a couple of bumbling cowboys when she had the whole world ahead of her? She was a beautiful, educated woman. They would only stifle her potential if they insisted she stay on their ranch. He felt like a fool.

"She'll be back," he said, his fire dashed. "Back...She'll be back...Back... Fuck!"

He didn't want to see the sympathy swimming in Arden's eyes. Not now. He turned away, still forced to repeat the words he knew were a lie.

Callum slammed the screen door shut after barreling into the kitchen. He was angry, defeated, and hurt. He'd allowed an outsider into his life, a woman. They'd laughed together, shared intimate moments, and she never judged him for his constant tics. She made him feel human, normal, and now she was likely on to bigger and better things. He felt smaller than a speck of flint.

Some days he was too weak or too tired to care about controlling the symptoms of his Tourette's. Right now he let it all go, embracing the anger and frustration. He kicked open his bedroom door and crashed onto his bed. He vowed never to leave his heart vulnerable again.

****

Hailey watched the road signs flash by her peripheral vision. The further they drove, the emptier she felt. *What have I done?*

"Mr. Fischer, I'm not sure I've made the right decision. I mean, it'll be like starting over—a new city, new apartment, new job."

"This is what you wanted, Ms. Watson. Sometimes you have to make the decision to advance your career, even if it's difficult. Being the daughter of two doctors, you should know the sacrifices required for a successful business."

She knew that they'd sacrificed family for money, love for their careers. Hailey had vowed never to become like them, but she was doing exactly that now, travelling to Jacksburg and kissing the O'Shea Ranch goodbye. *Money and success, or love?*

"Stop the car."

Her Professor made sure to remind her that she'd made the wrong choice. Even her friend Peter couldn't understand her devotion to the two misunderstood cowboys. They weren't evil. Despite the warnings, she trusted them enough to give up everything for a chance at a happily ever after.

She walked along the dusty side of the road, not even offered a ride back into the little town. Hailey remembered how Callum had rescued her and Arden. The difference in loyalty was night and day, and she knew she'd made the right decision.

Hailey still wanted to find out why Arden had sold his motorcycle. He was as passionate about that darned bike as she was about solving the hog problem. As she reached the periphery of town, she decided to stop at the distribution center to see if Arden's bike was still available. She'd find a way to get it back if she could.

Hailey thought things were doing well on the farm since Arden returned, but they must be worse off than she expected if he had to sell his prized bike to make ends meet.

Regardless of her choice to move to the city, Hailey was well aware she'd be receiving regular royalties for her contribution to the hog crisis. Her research was solid and even her Professors knew it.

Before she reached the center, a pickup truck pulled up alongside her.

"What's a nice girl like you doing walking out here alone?"

She turned to find Arden leaning out the passenger window, Callum at the wheel. Her dark-haired cowboys were a beautiful sight. Her throat clogged with emotion just seeing them.

"Well, I started down one road and realized it wasn't the one I should be following." She kept walking and the truck crawled along beside her.

"Really. So I take it you know which road you should be taking?"

"I do. Care to give me a ride?"

The truck stopped and the door opened. Callum didn't drive straight but veered off the road, bumping and jostling over the rough terrain.

When they were surrounded by fields, no sign of the road or civilization, Callum turned off the truck. The drone of crickets and cicadas filled the cab, a soothing lullaby. She was tired from a long, emotionally exhausting day and the long walk. The sky was transforming from blue to streaks of pink. The heat was dying down, making it the type of evening she'd love to spend on the wraparound porch with Callum and Arden. She couldn't imagine life without their stories, memories of their youth. They'd both come so far from the men she'd met only months earlier.

"Were you running away from us?" asked Arden. He wasn't angry, but they deserved honesty either way.

"I was chasing after dollar signs and recognition, but it's no different than trying to capture the wind. It slipped through my fingers, reminding me the only thing that will stand the test of time is love."

"Fancy words," said Arden.

"We can never offer you the things you can achieve in your career. We're from two different worlds. We're simple farmers, and you know what the townsfolk think of us," said Callum.

"I don't care," she said. Desperation crept up on her. He sounded final, as if he wasn't willing to give their relationship another try. The muscles around her heart felt like iron, each breath labored. She'd admitted to running from them. What if they decided they didn't want her back?

"So what're you saying, baby girl? You coming home with us?"

"If you'll have me."

Arden reached in his back pocket and pulled out a small, folded brown envelope.

"This is for you," he said, handing it to her.

She opened the envelope and a diamond engagement ring fell into her palm. Hailey stared at it for so long time seemed to stand still. It was perfect. She couldn't help but envision Callum and Arden picking it out, thinking of her. "What's this?"

"She's not very bright for a scientist," said Arden.

"Well, you're doing it all wrong," said Callum. "You have to put it on her finger all romantic-like."

Her eyes filled with unshed tears but she fought to keep them from falling.

Callum leaned over his brother's lap and took the

ring, slipping it onto her ring finger.

"It's–it's beautiful. But—"

"We want you to be ours, for now and always, Hailey Watson." Arden kissed her hand, studying the ring. "It looks beautiful on you."

"How did you afford this?"

"Darlin', you don't get how this thing works. You're supposed to say yes or no," said Arden. "Money ain't important."

She knew by the look in his blue eyes that he'd sold his bike to buy the ring. It was the only thing of value they could have sold. A tear slipped from her eye. "Yes! *Yes* to both of you and *yes* to always." Hailey had never been more certain of a decision in her life.

****

"Tighter," said Arden.

Callum tightened the ropes around her wrists, bringing her arms high above her head.

"At least close the loft doors," said Hailey. "Anyone can see me."

Callum laughed. "Darlin', you should know that nobody dares to venture on O'Shea land. Besides, you're our little wife now. We can do with you as we please."

They had their woman strung up in the hayloft, her arms bound and body stripped naked. She was a vision, his everything. Callum ran his hand through her hair as Arden spread her legs apart at the knees.

"No more," she begged. "I can't…"

"Hush, now. You lost the bet, so you have to endure two orgasms before we take you," said Callum.

Her chest heaved, her entire body flush with desire. A cooling breeze blew into the hayloft, making her skin break out in gooseflesh. It wouldn't be long and they'd have to prepare for the approaching winter. It was usually a sad time for Callum. He'd watch the leaves die off the trees as the land grew desolate and lifeless. He could already envision long nights in front of the fire— not in loneliness but with love and laughter. Callum had a family. The entire world could think he was a freak, but the only opinions that mattered were Arden's and Hailey's.

"Arden rigged the bet," she said, gasping when his brother descended on her clit. "His horse was better rested."

They'd had a good old-fashioned horse race across the plowed hay fields, and Arden won. The loser had to endure two orgasms before sex. As far as Callum knew, his brother never lost a horse race, and the trophies in his room were a testament to the fact.

Hailey knew what she was getting into. And he had a strong suspicion she enjoyed her punishment.

Callum kissed her lips, his hand roaming over her breasts. "I love you," he whispered in her ear. "You make me feel like a man." He wasn't good at sweet words or poetry. Even though it was difficult to express himself, he knew she understood. She made him feel special, and understood his syndrome and its many intricate layers. Hailey enjoyed studying him, hoping to contribute to finding a cure one day. She was just smart enough to surprise the world. And he loved it when she played doctor.

"*My* man," she murmured. "Don't let him torture me, Callum. Fuck me. Please."

Arden peered up at him from between her legs, his eyes narrowed.

Callum had given her the first orgasm in record time, and now it was Arden's turn. He'd be a fool to challenge his brother in the heat of the moment.

"Come for Arden, and then you can sit on my cock. You can ride me as hard and fast as you want."

"Callum…"

He helped her along, suckling her breasts as Arden brought her closer and closer to the edge. Her body convulsed, her hips lifting off the saddle blanket he'd set on the hay.

"Arden!" As she rode out her second orgasm, Callum watched her expressions. He loved everything about her from the spattering of freckles across her nose to the beauty marks on her neck. Her breasts jiggled as her body trembled, her hands tugging wildly at her binds.

When her body went limp, he used his pocket knife to cut the ropes securing her wrists. She immediately reached for him, wrapping her arms around his neck.

Arden climbed up to join them. They cocooned her between them, their combined heat staving off the fall chill.

Hailey was their woman. And now new memories would be created on the O'Shea Ranch. For the first time in his life, Callum couldn't help but smile when thinking of the future. It seemed God hadn't abandoned them, and even cowboy outcasts could attain a happily ever after.

The End

www.staceyespino.com

COWBOY OUTCASTS

EVERNIGHT PUBLISHING ®

www.evernightpublishing.com